The Man who Burned Hell!

The little town was Serenity: in name and nature. Then the railroad and miners came, dragging violence and death behind them. Renamed Hell, the sleepy town changed under the rule of Ike Cordis.

Known as The Devil, Cordis controlled The Three Horsemen, the fastest guns in town.

Long forgotten was the fourth horseman – a man riding a blue roan. A man determined to make The Devil burn in Hell!

The Man who Burned Hell!

Sam Clancy

A Black Horse Western

ROBERT HALE

© Sam Clancy 2018
First published in Great Britain 2018

ISBN 978-0-7198-2591-0

The Crowood Press
The Stable Block
Crowood Lane
Ramsbury
Marlborough
Wiltshire SN8 2HR

www.bhwesterns.com

Robert Hale is an imprint
of The Crowood Press

The right of Sam Clancy to be identified as
author of this work has been asserted by him
in accordance with the Copyright, Designs and
Patents Act 1988

Typeset by
Derek Doyle & Associates, Shaw Heath
Printed and bound in Great Britain by
CPI Group (UK) Ltd, Croydon, CR0 4YY

This one is for Sam and Jacob
and the old feller
Michael Hickmotte Towns

PROLOGUE

A bullet-riddled sign that had once read 'Serenity' stood on the outskirts of the town. The name had been crossed out with a slash of red paint and replaced by 'Hell' in crude hand-written letters. An apt name for the town it had become, rife with violent deaths and overseen by a man known as The Devil.

Three mounted horses thundered past the sign, covering it in a new layer of trail dust. The men rode hard towards the town, their eyes focused on a large pall of brown-black smoke that billowed upward, blotting out the pink and red streaks of the afternoon sky.

When they got closer, they could see large orange flames that leaped thirty feet into the air, fed by all manner of dry fuel.

The dust-covered men eased their sweat-lathered mounts to a halt when they hit the edge of town. They were presented with the conflagration responsible for the smoke and embers. On both sides of the street, buildings burned, the crackle and snap of tinder-dry planks could be heard over the roar of the fire.

'What happened here?' one of the men wondered

aloud as he tried to comprehend the sight before him.

'I'll kill him,' grouched their leader. 'Follow me.'

They dismounted and led their agitated horses along the main street, speaking reassuringly to them to allay their terror. They came across bodies, strewn haphazardly by the fickle hand of death, left in the very place that they had fallen.

Flames sucked the oxygen from the air and the oppressive heat felt suffocating as the men continued to walk, the bright silver of their marshal badges glinting in the glow.

To their left, a burning pile of rubble and part of a scorched sign that read 'Saloon' were all that remained of the formerly salubrious establishment. The rest of it was gone. To their right lay a wheel, some shattered timbers, and small black crater, which they discerned had once been some sort of wagon.

They continued their steady pace, one of them limping, a stunned silence hung over them at the awesome fury of the blaze. To them, it seemed that the entire town was on fire, except it wasn't. It was just the main street aflame; the other streets still untouched by the inferno.

Ahead of the small group, two figures appeared through the thick smoke. One was limping, holding what appeared to be a rifle while the second person struggled to support the first. As the three lawmen neared, it became apparent that the pair was a man and a woman. Apart from a blackened face, filthy clothes, and her wild, sooty red hair, the woman seemed fine.

The man she supported was dressed in black and it looked as though he hadn't fared as well. He had a bloody rag tied around his upper left thigh, a line of semi-dried blood had run down the left side of his unshaven face and he appeared to be wounded somewhere on his right side.

The three marshals stopped in their tracks and stared incredulously at the two people before them. The wounded man looked up and smiled wryly.

'Hey, Bass, where you been?'

United States Marshal Bass Reeves glared at Ford, and for a moment it was hard to tell which burned brighter: the town or the marshal's eyes. The muscles of his jaw clenched when he ground his teeth together as the rage within him reached boiling point. When he spoke, his voice held an edge that would shatter granite.

'What the *hell* have you done?'

CHAPTER 1

At birth, Serenity had been a cattle town, nestled in a wide valley with lush meadows, fast-flowing waterways fed from the high snow-capped peaks of the Absaroka Mountain Range, which overlooked its rutted main street.

Initially, that's all it was, a one-street town enclosed by false-fronted shops. With the passage of time, it grew and further streets were added. As the demand for a rail spur peaked, the railroad decided to build one into the valley so ranchers could ship out their cattle, making the need for a two-week drive to the closest railhead defunct.

Around the same time, the discovery of gold in the foothills drew miners in droves. Once it was established that the deposit was quite substantial, a mining company moved in and bought up the smaller claims.

Soon after that, Ike Cordis came to town with three hired guns – his Horsemen, as he liked to call them. They were cold-blooded killers who could draw and fire with speed and accuracy.

Sam Beck came from Texas, Colt Bliven from Kansas, and California Wells all the way from Sacramento.

Between them, they had a healthy kill tally of twenty-two.

Cordis quickly took over Serenity's saloon businesses. When he arrived in town, there were four: the Cattleman's Saloon, the High Valley, the Ace High, and the Buffalo Wallow. He immediately renamed them more to his liking. They became Ike's Place, the Pink Garter, the Dead Dog, and the Royal Palace. He kept them open all night; they never closed their doors. Not when there was so much money to be made.

With the influx of miners and rail workers came violence and death. Before long, not a day went by when there wasn't a shooting, a stabbing or a fight in the middle of town. Citizens were accosted in the main street as they went about their business. The Serenity sheriff did his best to enforce the law, but died after being shot in the back whilst doing his rounds late one evening.

And so, in the space of months, Serenity became a hell town where people lived hard and died violent deaths. The sign was changed from 'Serenity' to 'Hell' and people started to call Cordis 'The Devil', the king of Hell.

Three violent incidents occurred in one day that caused both Hell and The Devil to live up to their names. The first happened in the early morning hours. As a cold breeze whipped along the main street of Hell, the body of a man suspended from a rope began to sway. The noose around his thick neck had bitten deep into flesh, and after four hours beneath the Dead Dog saloon's sign, his face was distended and discoloured and his swollen tongue protruded from between slack lips.

As the body swung with the wind, the sun kissed a shiny object on the man's chest, and flashed briefly, though nobody was around to see it. The object was a nickel-plated

11

badge, a sheriff's badge, and its owner had only been in office since the previous day. His death was meant to serve as a warning to the town council not to interfere in The Devil's work.

The warning, however, was not heeded and the town council installed another man in his place as sheriff: a drifter who was offered three hundred dollars a month to wear the badge.

Within an hour of being sworn in, he died in a blaze of gun smoke, shot down by Sam Beck, one of Cordis' three Horsemen.

Thirty minutes later, the third violent event transpired that proved to be the beginning of the end for Hell.

A thick blue-grey smoke hung in the still air of the dimly lit back room of the Royal Palace. Its source was a fat cigar jammed between the teeth of Ike Cordis. A thin spiral left the end of the stogie as he drew back deeply, increasing the amount of stifling smoke in the enclosed space. He shuffled the deck of cards in his large hands then dealt to three people seated with him around the table.

Cordis was an imposing man in his mid-forties. At a little over six feet tall with a solid build, his confidence and bearing showed through his easy gait when he walked. His coal-black eyes were deep set below a broad forehead with a widow's peak hairline, and his jaw was square and strong. His partially grey hair was slicked back, exposing his deeply tanned face.

Strapped about his waist was a hand-tooled gun belt that held a piece with which he was very proficient, a Colt Peacemaker.

One of his acquaintances was Justus Harper, the local

12

mine boss. A bull of a man, Harper, also in his forties, had black hair and a face scarred from the many fistfights he'd participated in. Next was Isom Friend, the railroad boss. He was of a similar build to Harper, with brown eyes and red hair.

The final person at the table would have brightened any room with her presence. With her long black hair and low-cut red dress, Camilla turned heads wherever she went – mostly men's. The thirty-five-year-old was the owner of an establishment called the Joy Club, where she ran a stable of fifteen girls for her customers' entertainment.

Because of her beauty and lavish gowns, the tendency of most was to underestimate and deem her harmless, which was a mistake. Beneath her skirts, tucked into the garter on her right thigh was a Sharps four-barrel pistol. On the opposite leg, her garter held a short, bone-handled knife with a double-edged blade honed into a stiletto point. Many a man had tried to tame the raven-haired beauty; none had succeeded, and one had died.

'What do you have planned for when the spur is finished, Isom?' Cordis asked, around the stub of the cigar he chewed.

Friend scooped his cards up from the marked tabletop and looked them over. He didn't bother to look up. 'I guess wherever they send me.'

'How long did you say it would be until you're finished?'

'A couple of months.'

'I know a certain girl over at the Club who'll be sorry to see you go,' Camilla told him.

Friend thought of the redheaded Charley and felt his emotions stir.

'I know my billfold will be sorry to leave,' he deflected the comment.

For their part in a simple plan to drive business in the right direction, Friend and Harper received a percentage of profits made by the four saloons owned by Cordis, and the cathouse owned by Camilla. Come payday, the railroad and mine workers were paid in one of the saloons, where the first round of that day was free. Camilla sent her girls down to the saloons to work their marks and encourage them to return to the Club for alternative entertainment. It was simple, yet effective, and the money they were paid was quite a tidy sum.

'I know my profits will take a hit, that's for damned sure,' Cordis said. 'I might have to take up robbing some of them trains when they start running.'

No one at the table laughed because they knew that the likelihood of that happening was quite high. They all knew that he was behind the disappearance of a couple of gold shipments in the past.

Taking the cigar from his mouth, Cordis locked his gaze on Camilla. 'Are you staying over tonight or sleeping in your own bed?'

She gave him a mirthless smile. 'After the events of today, I think that perhaps your bed might prove a rather interesting place.'

Her gaze may have been on Cordis, but beneath the table, her foot rubbed teasingly at the inside of Friend's thigh. Camilla's sparkling eyes moved to the railroad boss and he shifted uncomfortably in his seat. Then she winked at him.

'I fold,' he blurted out, tossed his cards on the table and made to rise.

'Hold on!' Cordis snapped. 'We haven't even looked at our cards yet.'

'Let's just say I got me a feelin',' Friend said hurriedly.

Harper tossed his hand in too. 'Same goes for me. No offence, but you can't deal for horse crap.'

There was a knock at the door and a thin man with blond hair and blue eyes, aged in his early thirties, walked in.

'What is it, Sam?' Cordis asked.

Sam Beck was a killer for hire whose loyalty was to the person who paid him the most. He was Cordis' right hand, the Horseman turned to most frequently. Anything tough that needed to be taken care of was normally handled by Beck. Not that the other two weren't capable, but Cordis trusted Beck as much as one could trust a gun-for-hire.

'You said you wanted to know when the town council was cookin' somethin' up, well they're doin' it right now.'

Cordis reached up and removed the cigar stub with his forefinger and thumb. He spat a sliver of tobacco from his mouth and said, 'Are they now?'

'They're in the mayor's office as we speak.'

Cordis ran his eyes over the others at the table with him. He said, 'You would think that they would've learned by now.'

His face flushed with anger and he looked back at Beck and barked, 'Get the others! It's time to put a stop to this once and for all.'

'We need to stop Cordis, now!' the large, moon-faced man dressed in black bellowed.

'Shhh, keep it down, Willett. Someone will hear you,' rail-thin Dempsey Castner almost pleaded.

'I will not,' Mayor Willett Cowlin blustered from his seat. 'They've killed two town sheriffs in a matter of hours and something needs to be done about it.'

'We could send word to the marshal's office in Bismarck,' supplied Clarence Kile.

'We need to do something,' Cowlin confirmed to the rest of the town council. 'At this rate, the cemetery is growing faster than the town. We need to get rid of Cordis.'

As if on cue, the door to the mayor's office burst open and four men entered, led by Ike Cordis.

'I see you've started without me, Mayor Cowlin,' Cordis' voice dripped with sarcasm. 'Don't let us interrupt you. Please carry on.'

'What are you doing here, Cordis?' Cowlin snapped, even though his face had paled considerably. 'This is council business. You don't belong here.'

'Now I was of the opinion,' Cordis said, 'that anyone with a business in town could attend a meeting.'

'What could you possibly want at a town council meeting, Cordis?' Kile snorted.

A cold shiver ran down his spine as Cordis' icy gaze settled upon him. 'We thought that we should be present for the vote. After all, we are citizens of this fair town.'

'And what vote might that be?'

'Why, the one for the new mayor of course,' Cordis said jovially.

Cowlin was visibly shaken at the words uttered by Cordis and he didn't really want to know the answer to his next question. But he asked anyway. 'What new mayor?'

Cordis' voice hardened, 'Me.'

Beck pulled his six-gun and thumbed back the hammer.

The dry triple-click sounded unbelievably loud in the office. However, the roar of the shot seemed to tear the place apart.

The slug punched into Mayor Willett Cowlin's chest with the power of a sledgehammer. He was thrown back out of his chair and crashed to the floor in an untidy heap.

As the echo of the shot died away, Cordis looked at the horrified faces of those present in the room.

'It looks like the vote was unanimous,' the outlaw boss surmised. 'I guess I should take office immediately now that it's been vacated. Well, it will be once you remove the body. Anyone have a problem with that?'

The silence in the room was deafening.

'No? OK then. Let's get down to the first order of business. You're all fired.'

CHAPTER 2

When the plea for help caught up with United States Marshal Bass Reeves, he was in Billings, Montana with six other marshals. They were picking up notorious outlaw Mason Fox, who was to be transported to Lander, on the Popo Agie river, in Wyoming.

The numerous marshals were due to the fact that Fox's gang was still at large. There were eight of them and word was that they were in the area waiting to break him out.

Reeves was a man in his fifties, a hardnosed man who took no nonsense from anyone. His hair was greying and the change had drifted down to his mustache, giving it a salt and pepper look. His face was deeply lined and walnut brown, a legacy of his many years in the job that entailed running outlaws to ground.

There was a knock at Reeves' hotel door and a thin-faced man with a nickel-plated badge entered the small, dimly lit room.

'You got a minute, Bass?'

'What is it, Roy?' he asked Deputy Marshal Roy Willis.

Willis held up a slip of creased paper. 'This came for you.'

Reeves stood up from where he sat on the edge of his bed and reached for the message. While he read it through, noise from down on the main street drifted in through the open window.

'Has Josh turned up yet?' Willis asked.

He looked up at the deputy. 'No. Did you read this?'

Willis nodded. 'It sounds bad. Have you ever heard of this Serenity place?'

Reeves confirmed. 'There's been whispers about it. I was goin' to send a man to check it out a while back but the territorial governor got wind of it and told me not to worry. His words were, 'Let the local law deal with it'. I'm thinkin' now that I should've ignored him and went with my gut.'

'You do know that there is only one man for the job, don't you?' Willis pointed out. 'With a situation like this, he's probably the best one to deal with it.'

It pained Bass to think about it, but Willis was right. He needed the best man on his team for the job and that man was his son.

Reeves nodded. 'And if he ever shows up, I'll assign the job to him. I just wish I knew where he was.'

'You know Ford, Bass,' Willis commented, 'he's probably hip-deep in trouble.'

'Without a doubt, Roy. Without a doubt.'

Coyote Gibson smiled coldly and squeezed the trigger of his Colt, instantly killing the shotgun messenger where he stood beside the Billings' stage. The roar brought forth a stream of alarmed cries from the surviving driver and passengers.

The outlaws had stopped the stage on a level part of the trail, where both sides were strewn with rocks and trees. They'd dragged a deadfall across to create a blockage at the narrowest point. Once the concord was stopped, they ordered everyone on board to step down. Aside from the shotgun guard and driver, there were four passengers: two men and two women.

Gibson and both of his partners were callous killers, wanted in Montana, Wyoming, and Colorado on robbery and murder charges. One of those happened to be for a town sheriff who had tried to apprehend them on his own.

From beside the broad-shouldered, scar-faced outlaw, one of his men cackled. 'That'll teach the sumbitch to talk back to you, Coyote.'

'Just shut up and give Crick a hand to get that strong-box down, Bones,' Gibson snapped as he ran his eyes over the cowering passengers.

One passenger caught his eye; a pretty young redhead woman with pale skin and sparkling green eyes, with a slim figure clad in an emerald green dress. She held her head high, her jaw set firm, a defiant expression on her face. What intrigued him most was the fact that she hadn't blinked when faced with the cold-blooded murder of the guard.

'What's your name girl?' he growled at her.

'Eddie Yukon,' she snapped.

He looked at her thoughtfully. 'Are you scared, Eddie Yukon?'

'Not of you, I ain't.'

Surprised by her answer, Gibson asked, 'And why, pray tell, might that be?'

'Where I come from, scum like you are a dime a dozen.'

One of the other passengers gasped at her blatant disregard for their predicament. The driver whispered urgently, 'Take it easy, ma'am.'

'And where is it you come from?' Gibson pressed.

'Deadwood.'

'So, the tough little lady comes from a big tough town,' Gibson guffawed.

'Tough enough to chew a piece of horse dung like you up and spit you out,' Eddie hissed.

Gibson's eyes flared and he raised his gun. 'I wasn't goin' to kill you when I'm finished here. Not like the others. But I just changed my mind. I'll kill you first.'

Just as Gibson's knuckle whitened with the pressure of squeezing the trigger, a voice from behind him said, 'Is there a problem here?'

The stranger was dressed totally in black, from the brim of his low-crowned hat to the toes of his dusty boots. Even his gun belt was made of hand-tooled black leather. The big, blue roan horse he rode remained rock-steady, sensing the calmness of his rider.

The man's hat shaded his tanned face and the searching blue eyes of a man in his early thirties.

Gibson eyed him warily. 'If you want some advice, stranger, I'd move on if I were you.'

The rider chose to ignore the advice and climbed down from the horse, his back to Gibson, and removed his jacket, revealing a solid-built frame of just over six foot wrapped in a black shirt.

The outlaw leader frowned. 'Are you stupid or somethin'?'

The stranger turned around, the nickel-plated United

21

States Deputy Marshal's badge pinned to the left chest of his shirt, immediately evident. His hand dropped to the butt of his Colt Peacemaker.

From atop the stage, Gibson heard Bones say, 'Will ya get a look at that.'

'Are we goin' to do this the easy way, or the hard way?' the marshal asked in a casual tone.

'I'll be damned,' Gibson said. 'A lawdog.'

'Use it or drop it, Gibson.'

'So, you know who I am,' the outlaw mused. 'It seems to me that I'm at somewhat of a disadvantage.'

'The name's Ford. Josh Ford.'

There was a spark of recognition in the outlaw's eyes and that was all Ford needed to spring into action. With blinding speed, the Peacemaker came out of its holster and roared. Gibson's head snapped back violently as the .45 caliber slug punched into his skull and blew his brains out a hole in the back of his head.

Ford shifted his aim and fired twice more. Atop the coach, the outlaw known as Bones screamed in pain when both slugs smashed into his chest. Almost gracefully, he fell from his elevated position and landed unceremoniously with a thud on the dusty trail.

The third outlaw, Crick, brought up an old Remington six-gun and snapped off a panicked shot at Ford. It whined harmlessly off into the surrounding brush. The Peacemaker in the marshal's fist spat lead once more and the final outlaw died with a bullet in his chest.

A thin wisp of blue-grey gun smoke spiraled lazily from the barrel of Ford's six-gun as he reloaded. He turned to look over the passengers who stood beside the coach, seemingly in shock.

'Is everybody all right?' he asked.

The grey-headed driver with a handlebar mustache stepped forward. 'I – I think so. Except for poor Jim there.' He indicated the dead messenger on the ground. 'He had a wife and two young'uns.'

Ford nodded. 'A man like that ought not be ridin' guard on a stage. He should have a permanent town job.'

He looked each passenger over until his eyes settled on Eddie Yukon. 'And you, Miss, have a big mouth.'

Her jaw dropped and her pale face flushed with anger. Ford cut her off before she could say anything. 'One thing you need to learn is you don't go pokin' a bear like Coyote Gibson and expect to get away with it. He paid no never mind to any of the people he killed. Men or women, it was all the same to him. Just you remember that.'

'I guess I should thank you then,' Eddie acquiesced.

'Just remember it the next time you get held up on a stage. I might not be around to save your ass.'

The look she gave him was that of indignation. One thing he realized about her: unlike the other female on the stage, she showed no effects of the violence that had passed. Maybe she was tough. She certainly was pretty.

'I take it you're all headed into Billings?' Ford asked the driver.

'Yes, sir.'

'Get everythin' sorted out. I'll ride with you.'

The main street of Billings was playing host to a macabre procession that ended outside the jail. A large crowd of onlookers lined both sides of the thoroughfare as Ford passed through; the only things missing were cheers and bunting or it could be mistaken for a festive occasion. He

23

led the outlaws' horses loaded with their stiffening bodies draped over them.

Across the street, Bass Reeves stood on the rough-plank boardwalk outside of the hotel, along with two other marshals: Willis, and a big man called Crown.

'This is becomin' a habit,' Reeves growled in a low voice. 'They'll treat him like some kinda hero now and worship the ground he walks on. He is only doin' his job.'

'C'mon, Bass,' Crown said, 'even you gotta admit he's good at what he does.'

'Yeah, and one of these days he won't be and it'll get him killed,' Reeves snapped.

'What's the problem, Bass?' Willis asked. 'Is it that he takes unnecessary risks, or is it because he reminds you of yourself?'

Reeves' gaze hardened. 'Go and rescue him from that mob before I send you to Serenity in his place.'

He turned around and walked back into the hotel to wait for his son.

Wilson, on the other hand, stepped down off the boardwalk and started across the street. Once he'd reached the crowd he pushed his way through until he broke out the other side and found Ford standing beside his roan.

'I see you've been busy,' Willis commented. 'Who are they?'

'Coyote Gibson and his no-good friends,' Ford answered. 'Did I see Bass standin' over on the boardwalk when I rode in?'

Willis nodded.

'I guess he was his usual cheery self?'

'He has a problem that he needs you to deal with,'

24

Willis explained. 'He wants to see you over at the hotel.'

'I thought we were all gatherin' here to escort Mason Fox over to Lander?'

'Somethin's come up that needs immediate attention,' Willis told him. 'Your old man'll explain.'

Ford nodded. 'I'll put the roan up at the livery then come right over.'

'I'll let him know,' Willis said. 'And good work with Gibson, by the way.'

'That wasn't work,' Ford told him. 'It was a pleasure.'

'It's about time you showed up,' Reeves growled. 'Close the door behind you.'

'It's good to see you too, Bass,' Ford greeted him, sarcasm evident in his voice.

The pair may have been tied together by blood, but not by name. Reeves had left Josh and his mother when Ford was just a boy, and gone off to fight in the war and never returned. After the death of his mother, Ford had taken his mother's maiden name, and set out to find the man who'd abandoned them, determined to kill him.

Instead, when he'd found Bass, Ford joined the marshals and become one of their top law enforcement officers.

Ford looked at Willis then back to his father. 'Roy mentioned there was a job that's come up.'

Reeves nodded. 'Ever heard of a place called Serenity?'

'Not sure.'

'What about a feller called Ike Cordis?'

'Nope.'

'Sam Beck, Colt Bliven, California Wells?'

'Sam Beck and California Wells I've heard of,' Ford

allowed. 'The other feller I ain't. Beck's a real killer. He'd shoot down anyone if the price was right. Why all the questions?'

'I got a message from a member of the now defunct town council of Serenity. It seems that Cordis has installed himself as mayor of the town after Beck killed his predecessor.'

'Why don't the local law arrest him?' Ford asked.

'There is no local law,' Reeves explained. 'Cordis had him killed as well. And apparently, an hour after the new sheriff was sworn in, he too was killed.'

'What's so important about this Serenity place anyway that it warrants all these killin's?'

'At the moment the place is a hotbed of money,' Reeves said. 'The railroad is buildin' a spur into town for the cattlemen and the miners are pullin' a fortune out of the ground. Accordin' to the message I got, Cordis is in league with the railroad boss, the mine boss, and the local brothel owner.'

Reeves paused before he said, 'A woman called Camilla.'

Recognition flared in Ford's eyes. He opened his mouth to speak but Reeves stopped him.

'Just haul back on them reins a minute, Josh. It may not be her.'

'I guess we'll find out.'

Reeves nodded, remembering the last time Ford had crossed paths with Camilla.

'After we've delivered Fox to Lander, we'll swing by and see how you're getting' on.'

'What do you want me to do, Bass?'

'Take over the law, recruit yourself some deputies, and

clean the place up,' Reeves said sternly. 'Watch yourself, Josh. They're callin' Cordis "The Devil".'

'Well, I guess that puts me one step ahead in the game then, don't it?' Ford told his father. 'Not bein' a religious man, I don't believe in such things.'

CHAPTER 3

Four days after his departure from Billings, when the sun was still near its zenith, Ford sat atop his mean-tempered blue roan staring at the bullet-pocked sign. Someone had crossed out the word 'Serenity' and replaced it with 'Hell'!

'Looks like we've arrived, horse,' Ford surmised. 'I guess we'd best go and see if it's as bad as they say.'

Before easing the roan forward along the deeply rutted trail, Ford swept back the right flap of his coat to reveal the Colt Peacemaker. He unhitched the hammer thong so it wouldn't inhibit swift use should it be called upon. Then, with pressure from his knees, he sent the horse on its way into town.

Serenity consisted of seven streets. The main street, plus a parallel one either side, and four cross streets. On the eastern side of town, construction of the new railroad station was forging ahead, and nearing completion were large holding pens for the cattle that would be shipped when the line was finished.

Every so often a hollow boom could be heard from the north of the town where blasting was taking place in the foothills at the Gold Nugget mine.

With the livery stable at the far end of town, Ford had a chance to observe Serenity/Hell. The main street was called Absaroka, named for the range that overlooked the town, and as Ford rode along it he noticed that nearly every building had a large false-front attached. There were four saloons, a cattleman's office, two hotels, the general store, a mines office, lands office, plus any number of other businesses that folks needed for daily life.

He made note of the local newspaper and decided to pay it a visit after he settled in. As he rode past the jail he noticed that it had fresh boards across the doorway and large front window. A sign painted on one of the boards was clearly visible: 'Closed!'

A flurry of gunfire from the last saloon he passed brought forth a high-pitched scream, followed by a string of curses. Citizens scattered at the sound, before two large men emerged from the Royal Palace carrying the body of a black suited figure and callously dumped it off the edge of the plank boardwalk.

Ford's hand dropped to the butt of his Colt as one of the men looked up at him riding past. The deputy recognized him straight away. He was Raven Morris, hired gun and back-shooter. The killer stared at Ford briefly then turned around and walked back inside.

He continued until he reached the livery. It was a sizable building with double doors and a hayloft above the entrance. That, however, did not hold his attention. Beside the livery stood a double-storey, false-fronted building with a second-floor balcony and large mullioned windows.

The front was painted a pale pink, and above the second-storey windows was a large hand-painted sign, which read 'The Joy Club'.

He was drawn toward it – he needed to know. The roan made the decision for him and walked through the double-doors of the livery.

Ford walked along the boardwalk towards the second hotel he'd sighted on his ride through town. If he remembered correctly, it was called the Mountain View. His saddle-bags were slung over his left shoulder and his Winchester '76 was gripped in his right hand.

There was a commotion on the boardwalk ahead and a group of townsfolk quickly parted to allow a burly looking man with a beard through, before he could push them out of his way. He looked at Ford and said in a harsh tone, 'Get outta the way, bum.'

Stopping in the centre of the timber thoroughfare, Ford planted his feet shoulder width apart. The thug pulled up suddenly and glared at him. 'Are you deaf or somethin'?'

'Say please,' Ford demanded.

'What?'

'I said, "say please".'

The expression on the man's face became a snarl. He went to shove Ford out of the way but the marshal brought up the Winchester and drove its barrel into his ample middle. The thug doubled over, gasping for breath. Ford then raised the rifle and brought the butt down on the back of the man's head, dropping him instantly where he remained still.

All about Ford, townsfolk looked stunned at the swift decisiveness of his actions. He took in the wide-eyed stares, then shrugged his shoulders and continued along the boardwalk until he found the hotel.

He pushed in through the glass panel doors and crossed the hardwood boards, his heels clunking with each step. When he reached the registration counter, he stopped and looked about. There appeared to be nobody about so he picked up the small bell and rang it. A tinny tinkling filled the foyer and died away when Ford returned the bell to the counter.

He was impressed by the cleanliness of the lobby, the floors neatly swept and the counter was free of dust and polished to a high sheen. The glass in the entrance door and the front windows were clean as well.

He heard footsteps on the landing above him, and a middle-aged man with greying hair appeared and clomped down the stairs.

'Sorry to keep you waiting,' he apologized. 'My name is Borden. How can I help you?'

'I'd like a room for a few nights if you have one?'

'Sure, I've a room upstairs. It is away from the street so it should be reasonably quiet for you,' he told Ford.

'I'd prefer a room overlookin' the street,' Ford informed him.

'I'm sorry but the last one went a while ago to another gentleman,' the clerk said. 'I'm expecting him back soon. He just went to the Royal Palace to do something and said he'd be right back.'

'This feller wasn't wearin' a black suit of clothes, was he?' Ford asked, remembering the dead man whose body had been dumped on to the street.

'Why, yes, he was.'

Ford nodded. 'Fine, I'll take his room. He ain't comin' back.'

'How can you be so sure?' Borden asked.

'Because he's dead. Not long back I saw a couple of fellers dump him outside of the saloon you mentioned.'

Borden paled. 'Oh, Lord. Another one. That makes three this week, and it's only Tuesday.'

'Does it happen often?' Ford asked as he signed the register.

'Too often, Mr . . .' he looked at the register. 'Mr Ford. It happens all too often.'

'You wouldn't know where I could find a feller by the name of Clarence Kile, would you?' Ford asked, using the name that Bass had told him.

Once again Borden's face betrayed his emotions. 'He – he owns the local store not much further along the street.'

'If I slip along and see him now will that give you enough time to sort that room out the dead feller won't be needin' anymore?' Ford inquired.

Borden nodded jerkily. 'I'll see to it.'

'Good,' Ford said, heaving his saddle-bags on to the counter top. 'Put those in the room while you're at it and I'll pay when I come back.'

'Umm . . .' Borden hesitated.

'What is the problem?' Ford asked him.

He turned a shade of red with embarrassment and asked, 'You couldn't pay for the room beforehand, could you? Just in case something happens to you.'

Ford's face remained deadpan as he said, 'If somethin' happens to me then I won't be needin' it, will I? I'll pay when I return.'

Borden opened his mouth to protest but Ford was gone.

*

The interior space of Kile's Emporium was much larger than you might have expected it to be, judging from outward appearances. The narrow frontage belied an elongated room with no windows and no natural light. Dim lamps provided poor illumination within the cramped shop. When Ford opened the door, a small bell jingled, announcing his arrival.

As he moved towards the counter at the rear of the store a voice called out, 'We're closed.'

Ford kept walking down the narrow aisle, with each side crammed with clothes, foodstuffs, leather goods, and hardware items. When he reached the timber counter at the rear of the store, he saw three men in a space off to the right, not visible from the doorway. Two of them were big and burly, wore patterned shirts and worn britches tucked into high-topped boots. They stood on either side of the third man in an aggressive manner.

The object of their attention wore grey suit pants, and a white shirt stained with blood. His salt and pepper hair was slicked over with some manner of hair cream.

'I said we're closed,' the front man said.

Shaking his head, Ford complained, 'I can't believe this town, I surely can't. I ride into town and the first thing I see is some poor feller being dumped out on to the street. Dead! Then I'm walking along the boardwalk towards the hotel, mindin' my own business, and some hillbilly thinks it would be good to stomp me into the ground. Then I come here and what do I find?'

Ford paused for effect before continuing. 'You two deadbeats beatin' up on the storekeeper. Now tell me, what is wrong with this place?'

'What did you call us?' the front man growled.

'I'm sorry, are you fellers deaf as well as stupid?' Ford's voice dripped with sarcasm.

The front man's face flushed with anger and he stalked towards Ford, flexing his fingers. 'You'll be sorry for that.'

Now, it's an unwise man who goes up against two larger men without a plan. And although it wasn't the first time Ford had done such a thing, this time he had a plan, hastily constructed though it was, and it sat in a barrel beside his right hand.

A hickory axe handle came up in a deadly arc and the sound of wood connecting with bone cracked throughout the store like a gunshot. The thug had no time to react due to the sudden nature of the swing. One minute he was on his feet, the next he was laid out at Ford's.

The deputy marshal looked up at the second thug. 'Are you goin' to make the same mistake as your friend here?'

'I'm goin' to kill you, stranger,' the man hissed as he advanced on Ford.

Ford shrugged and prepared to meet his adversary. 'Your mistake to make, friend.'

With the bully within reach, Ford drove the axe handle at his face, butt-end forward. In a spurt of blood, his nose was smashed, stopping him in his tracks. Ford lowered the handle and drove it forward again, doubling the man over.

The thug sank to his knees in front of Ford and the deputy studied the moaning man briefly. Ford wound up again and broke the hickory handle over the man's head, cutting short the moans and causing him to topple on to his side.

'What have you done?' the storekeeper blurted out, fear evident in his voice.

'Are you Kile?' Ford asked.

'You need to leave,' he said, ignoring the question.

'Are you Kile?' Ford asked again, more forcefully this time.

'Yes, now leave before those men wake up.'

'Wait here,' the deputy ordered as he bent down and grabbed the first thug by his collar.

Ford dragged him up the narrow aisle and out the door, heaving him off the edge of the boardwalk. He then turned and walked back inside. 'Seems to me it's what they do with unwanted things around here.'

He repeated his actions with the second bully before returning to Kile who stood with his mouth agape, trying to process what had just happened. Ford pulled back the lapel of his jacket and revealed his United States Deputy Marshal's badge.

'I believe you sent for me,' Ford said, letting the flap fall back.

'Oh, good Lord. You're a marshal?'

'Uh-huh.'

'You need to be careful, he has eyes everywhere,' Kile warned.

'Who?'

'The Devil – I mean Cordis.'

'Can you get the rest of your town council together for a meeting tonight?' Ford asked him.

Kile stopped dabbing at his bloody face with a rag and looked at Ford, uncertainty in his eyes. 'I can, but you should know that the last time that happened, Cordis got wind of it and killed the mayor.'

'You let me worry about that,' Ford assured him. 'I have a room over at the Mountain View. Have them there around eight.'

Kile opened his mouth to speak when the doorbell rang out. The steady rhythm of clomping footsteps on the floorboards grew louder as someone approached. Kile gave Ford an alarmed look when the newcomer appeared. It was Sam Beck.

CHAPTER 4

The blond-headed killer stopped and looked the two men over thoughtfully with his cold blue eyes. Kile shifted nervously under the watchful gaze.

'Havin' some trouble, Kile?' Beck asked.

'No – no, no trouble.'

Beck's eyes moved across to Ford. 'That's funny. Them two miners outside said there was a stranger come in here and carved them up with an axe handle. You wouldn't know anythin' about that, would you?'

'I guess when you play a dangerous game like them, you're bound to meet somebody better,' Ford interjected.

Beck nodded. 'Comes with the territory, so they say.'

'So they say,' Ford agreed coolly.

'Are you stayin' around town long?' Beck asked.

'A couple of days.'

'It's a mighty rough place to stop over, friend,' Beck warned. 'Might pay to move on before you step in somethin' you can't scrape off your boot.'

A mirthless smile split Ford's face. 'That's mighty neighbourly of you. I'll take it under advisement.'

Beck stared at Ford, wondering if he was slow or just

plain ignorant. Instead, he shrugged his shoulders and said, 'Suit yourself. But don't say you weren't warned.'

'I'll be fine. Thanks for your concern.'

Shaking his head, Beck turned around and walked out of the store.

'Why didn't you tell him you're a marshal?' Kile blurted out after the killer had left.

'He didn't ask,' Ford said before his gaze hardened and his voice grew an edge. 'Don't you say anythin' either. I'll let people know in my own way. As of this minute, you're the only one who knows that I am. If I hear any different, I'll know where it has come from.'

'I – I won't say a word.'

'Good. Keep it that way. I'll see you in my room tonight. Number . . .'

He remembered that he didn't have a room number. 'Ask the clerk when you get there. Right now, I have somewhere else to be.'

Ten minutes later saw Ford in the newspaper office talking to Thornton Kinsey, the editor. He was a round-faced man with dark hair and glasses.

'What can I do for you, Mr Ford?' he inquired without looking up from his printing press.

'I'd like you to print me up some fliers.'

'Sure,' Kinsey said and walked across to his desk. He picked up a pencil stub and a piece of paper and put it on the timber counter in front of Ford. 'Write down what you want to say.'

He left the deputy to it and went back to the task at hand. After a couple of minutes, Ford said, 'I'm done.'

Kinsey came back to the counter, picked up the paper

and looked it over. His eyes lifted from it and peered over his glasses. 'Do you have the authority to do this?'

Ford showed him the badge pinned to his chest.

'OK, then I'll rephrase my question: do you really want to do this? You're bound to upset a lot of people when this goes up,' he said as he waved the piece of paper.

'You let me worry about that,' Ford told him. 'Can you have them done by tomorrow afternoon?'

'Sure.'

'And one more thing. Don't say anythin' to anyone. I'm not ready for it to come out yet. I still need to meet with the town council.'

'My lips are sealed.'

Ford's room at the hotel was small. There was space enough for the iron-framed bed, a nightstand with a dish and water jug on it for washing up, a single chair, and not much else. The walls were papered in a plain pattern, but the window overlooked the street as he'd requested.

The four remaining men of the town council, Kile, Mercier, Castner, and Carruthers, were squeezed into his room. Each one of them looked nervous.

'This is a bad idea,' a sullen looking Mercier whined. 'A very bad idea.'

'The door's there if you want to leave,' Ford told him. 'I appreciate that this is a dangerous situation and I won't think any less of you if you choose that option. That goes for all of you.'

The four men glanced at each other to see if any of them would leave. However, all remained where they were.

'Good,' Ford said. 'I'm having fliers put up that put all the saloons and the whore house on notice that they must close by midnight.'

There was a murmur from the men.

'What seems to be the problem with that?' Ford asked.

'You can't expect that to be enforced,' Kile said.

'Why not?'

'Because you're only one man,' Castner pointed out the obvious.

Ford looked at the thin man. 'A good point you make, Mr Castner. However, you fellers from the town council are goin' to find me two deputies from your town who have got sand enough to back my play. I want men that'll kill without hesitation should the need arise. The last thing I need is a man watching my back who is too afraid to pull the trigger.'

'You have to understand, Marshal, what you're asking is almost impossible,' Mercier told him.

'Why?' Ford snapped.

'Because after what happened to the previous town-appointed lawmen, no one wants to do it.'

'I don't care what you have to do, find someone who's willin' to do the job,' the tone in Ford's voice was menacing.

'OK, OK. Ease up,' Kile said, trying to ease some of the tension in the air. 'I'll find someone myself.'

They spent the rest of the time talking about Cordis' arrival in Serenity and what had happened to the previous law appointments. Once they were finished, Ford was confident that he knew all he needed to.

'The first step will be gettin' me the deputies and the second is the fliers goin' up. That should show them we mean business.'

'What is the third step?' Kile asked tentatively.

Ford smiled. 'We slay the Devil.'

A commotion on Absaroka Street woke Ford around one in the morning. He came off his bed and padded over to the window where silver moonlight flooded in, bathing the room with a pale glow that illuminated his scarred, muscular torso. He looked down on to the street and could make out two men working over another with fists and boots.

Ford hurried back to his bed, pulled his pants on and sat down. He pulled his boots on to his feet then buckled on his Colt .45. Before leaving his room, he scooped up the Winchester and levered a round into its breech. By the time he reached the street, the two assailants were gone, leaving the man who'd been on the receiving end lying on the ground.

Ford knelt beside the man and asked, 'Are you OK, pard?'

The man groaned. 'I'm OK. Been stomped worse by a steer.'

'Can you stand up?'

After a minute or so the man managed to get his feet beneath him and stood erect. He patted his pockets and looked at Ford, one eye already closing.

'Bastards took my money,' he slurred through split lips.

'How much did they get?'

'Ten bucks,' he answered. 'It was all I had.'

'Who were they? Why'd they beat you up like that?' Ford inquired.

'They're enforcers from the Dead Dog saloon. I complained about the roulette wheel and they didn't like it,' he explained. 'The sonsofbitches have it rigged.'

41

'What's your name?'

'Alec Potts,' the man said.

'I'm Ford.'

There was an outburst of laughter along the far board-walk and Ford saw the two men standing in the yellow glow of light coming from the saloon's large front window. He got to his feet and growled, 'Wait here.'

'What are you doin'?' Potts asked.

'I'm goin' to get your money back,' Ford told him.

'Hell, Ford. It's only ten bucks. It ain't worth dyin' over.'

'Who said anythin' about dyin'?'

Potts watched as Ford walked towards the saloon. No shirt and the Winchester in his right hand.

'Good luck,' Potts murmured.

Inside the den of iniquity called the Dead Dog, the noise was almost deafening. Drunks shouted out across the room, an out-of-tune piano was belting out 'Oh Susannah', and every now and then a piercing squeal of delight from one of the girls Camilla supplied from the Joy Club cut across the top of it all.

Tobacco smoke hung thick in the air and the rank smell of unwashed bodies became cloying in the close press of the gathered crowd. Here and there an argument flared only to be put down by one of the four burly enforcers hired for that purpose. However, these men were known to do more than just keep the peace in the saloon. On more than one occasion, some unlucky soul had died at their hands too.

Behind the bar were two keeps working hard to keep the drinks up to their clientele, their white cloths moving swiftly over the counter top between customers. Out in the back room, the manager of the Dead Dog was being entertained by a young lady named Candy.

The roulette table was surrounded by miners and railway workers, while the poker tables took most of the pay of many others.

The general atmosphere in the premises was jovial until it all went to hell when a man smashed inwards through the large front window. He landed with a resounding thump on the timber floor, shards of glass raining down around and upon him. A screech from one of the whores echoed throughout the saloon when she was sprayed with glass.

On the boardwalk, outside the now vacant window cavity, lay another man. He writhed in pain from the broken jaw he'd just received. Standing over him was a shirtless man holding a Winchester.

The saloon manager, Ely Cramer, stormed from the back room but pulled up short when he saw the devastation before him. Two of his enforcers were down and the other two had taken up place like sentries guarding the gaping hole in the front wall.

'What the hell is going on here?' he shouted across the room.

As he strode forward, the throng of people parted to allow his passage. He stopped short of the busted window and locked his angry gaze on to Ford.

'Well? Care to tell me what the hell happened?'

Casually, Ford stepped through the cavernous space into the room, glass crunching under his heeled boots. He walked towards Cramer and stopped.

'Your bullyboys were beatin' up on a feller on the street,' he informed the manager. 'It seemed that

43

someone took exception to him claimin' that the roulette wheel was rigged.'

A murmur ran through the saloon at the claim. A look of alarm flashed across Cramer's face but was quickly replaced by a look of indignation.

'We run clean games here, stranger,' he snapped. 'I'll not have you spouting anything to the contrary.'

Ford ignored him. 'They didn't stop there, though. They stole his money. It weren't much, only ten dollars, but to him, it was all he had.'

'And you did all of this just for that?'

Ford shrugged. 'It's the principle of the matter.'

Cramer looked at his two enforcers and snarled, 'Get him out of here!'

The rifle in Ford's hands came up. 'You boys take a step and this time I'll plant someone.'

They darted furtive glances at their boss who nodded and waved them away.

'Smart move.'

'What is it you want? The money?' Cramer asked.

Ford shook his head. 'Nope, I already got that. But I would like to have a look at that roulette wheel of yours.'

'I don't think so,' a harsh voice cut in.

The speaker stepped forward. He was a tall man with eyes the same colour as his dark brown hair. His six-gun was tied down low on his left side and Ford changed his rifle over to free up his gun arm.

'Where the hell have you been, Colt?' Cramer snapped.

'Not far,' Bliven answered casually. His attention turned back to Ford. 'The name's Colt Bliven. I work for Ike Cordis. He owns this establishment. Do you still want to look at that roulette wheel?'

44

'Oops,' Ford said, feigning shock. 'You work for Mr Cordis?'

Bliven nodded.

'I guess there's been some kind of mistake then,' Ford stated.

Smiling coldly, Bliven said, 'Maybe.'

'And you made it,' Ford said in an icy tone. 'Now get the hell away from me.'

Several emotions crossed Colt Bliven's face as he processed Ford's words. He finally settled on anger and his face turned scarlet.

A deathly silence descended over the room. No one had ever challenged one of Ike Cordis' Horsemen before, let alone to this extent. The anticipation began to build, of the impending death of the shirtless stranger.

Those who had not witnessed the gun speed of Colt Bliven had heard about it, but none were prepared for what happened next.

Bliven's left hand slashed down and clawed at the butt of his six-gun. As it came out and up, the gunfighter thumbed back the hammer ready to fire when it snapped into line. It never made it that far because two slugs from Ford's Peacemaker slammed into Bliven's chest just left of center.

The killer staggered back a step, red blossoms on the front of his shirt. Ford thumbed back the hammer on his six-gun once more and fired. This time the bullet smashed into Bliven's skull and blew his brains out the back of his head.

Every onlooker was stunned into silence. Ford replaced the empties in his Colt and holstered it. He looked at Cramer and said, 'Show me your roulette wheel.'

Cramer looked up from the body of Colt Bliven and swallowed hard. He pointed to the left side of the room and said, 'It's over there.'

One of the enforcers took a step forward but the Winchester in Ford's grip moved to cover him. 'No need for you to be movin',' Ford warned him. 'Just stay there and you might get to see the sun come up.'

The deputy marshal walked over to the roulette wheel, all eyes in the room locked on his every move. He looked it over briefly, spun it once with the ball and waited until it stopped. He looked at a man who had been playing and handed him the Winchester. 'Hold this.'

Ford then picked up an empty chair and brought it crashing down. It splintered like matchwood and broke the roulette wheel beyond repair. He dropped what was left of the chair on the sawdust-covered floor and retrieved his gun from the gambler. He turned to face the room.

'My name is Josh Ford!' he addressed them in a loud voice. 'I'm a United States Marshal, and the new law in Serenity. From now on what I say goes. Make the most of tonight, because come tomorrow, there's goin' to be some changes.'

Ford turned his gaze on Cramer and indicated to Bliven's corpse. 'Clean up your mess.'

Without another word, Ford left the Dead Dog and walked out on to the street where Potts still waited.

'I seen it all from here,' he said excitedly. 'Through the window.'

Ford passed him a rolled-up bundle of cash. Potts took it and said, 'Thanks, but there's too much money there. They only took ten.'

'Keep it,' Ford told him. 'How would you like a job?'

Potts couldn't help but show surprise. 'I have one. I work for one of the ranches here abouts.'

'What do you earn? Thirty?'

'Yeah.'

'How about fifty a week?'

'Doin' what?'

'Be my deputy.'

Potts looked at him. 'Deputy at what?'

'I'm a marshal,' Ford explained.

Potts' eyes grew wide. 'Oh, you want me to become your deputy so I get shot at instead of you?'

'Somethin' like that,' Ford said, half smiling.

'Give me sixty a week and you got yourself a deal.'

'Understand this, there is a good chance you could get killed,' Ford explained.

'I been here from the start,' Potts said. 'I seen what Cordis and the others have done to this town and you are the first feller to come along that looks like he stands a chance against these killers.'

'It could get worse before it gets better.'

'I'm in.'

'Fine. I'll see you in the mornin'. Come to the Mountain View around nine.'

'See you then.'

Ford watched him go and hoped that Potts hadn't just signed his death warrant.

47

CHAPTER 5

In its heyday, the Royal Palace had been a lavishly furnished saloon with a large crystal chandelier hanging from its ceiling. Its opulence was unmatched by anything far and wide. The wooden wall panels were burnished to a deep lustre, and the highly polished counter matched the tabletops. It also had a carpet runner that ran up the center of the stairs leading to the first-floor landing. A large mirror had adorned the wall behind the bar and a long brass footrail had run the length of the bar, hence the change of name from the Buffalo Wallow to something more befitting its grandeur when Cordis came to town.

During the short time that had elapsed since the change of ownership, most of the décor of the establishment had changed also. The chandelier had been shot down by a drunk, the wall panels were riddled with bullet holes, and the tables and countertop had lost their sheen and were badly marked. The Royal Palace certainly wasn't royal anymore.

It was here that Sam Beck found Ike Cordis. The outlaw leader was sitting in a corner of the near empty saloon eating ham and eggs. Beck sat down on the opposite side of the table and said, 'I suppose you heard what happened last night?'

Cordis nodded and forked another load of food into his mouth.

'What do you want to do about it?'

Cordis waited until he'd finished chewing before he answered. 'Observe.'

Beck frowned. 'What do you mean, "observe"? He killed Colt. I met him in the store yesterday after he put down two miners. He's a cool one. He won't scare easy and he's goin' to cause us more trouble than you can poke a stick at.'

'I want to see what our new-found friend has in store for the town,' Cordis explained. 'I don't want to go starting a full-scale war with the United States Marshals if I can avoid it. Killing local law is one thing, but killing a federal man could bring a whole world of grief down upon us. If we wait and see, the problem might just go away by itself.'

'And if it don't?' Beck asked.

'Then he'll have to go,' Cordis said. 'But we'll have to be smart about it. We don't want his death comin' back to us.'

'Have you ever heard of Ford, Ike?' Beck asked.

Cordis was busy working on another mouthful of his breakfast and just shook his head.

'I have,' the gunfighter said. 'He's a real wildcard. The marshals give him the tough jobs that need doin'. A while back he took down Mordecai Wakefield and his bunch. There was over a dozen of them. Until Ford was sent in, they'd killed two marshals.'

Cordis swallowed his food and said, 'You make him

sound invincible, Sam.'

The gunfighter shook his head. 'I'm just sayin' he'll need close watchin' is all.'

'Well, while you're watching our friend, find out who sent for him,' Cordis told Beck. 'Someone had to have sent word to the marshals otherwise he wouldn't be here. Once you find out, let me know.'

'OK, sure.'

Cordis pointed at his plate. 'Do you want something to eat?'

Beck stood up to leave. 'Nope, I'll catch up with you later.'

'Where are you going?'

'To observe.'

Ford and Potts stood on the boardwalk opposite the jail and did some watching of their own, that following morning. This time, however, Ford was fully clothed. Potts was too, but he bore the scars of the previous night. His eye was black and swollen, leaving only a slit to see through. His lips were puffy and scabbed over.

'Maybe you should wait a couple of days before you start work,' Ford had suggested but Potts refused.

So here they were, observing.

'Do you get the feelin' that everyone is lookin' at us?' Potts asked, as a well-dressed couple strode past, staring them up and down.

'I'm used to bein' stared at,' Ford allowed. He looked both ways along Absaroka Street and noted a few persons of interest, Sam Beck being one of them.

Ford reached up and touched his hat brim, letting the killer know that he knew. Beck nodded.

The deputy sighed. 'C'mon Potts, let's get this jail open.'

For the next ten minutes or so, the noise of splintering wood echoed around the immediate vicinity of the jail as the planks were removed from the window and door.

Inside the jail, a thin film of dust covered almost everything. The chair behind the desk was on its side and the gun rack was empty. The peg where the keys were kept was the same and Ford guessed that the cells in the back room were locked. He was right.

'I guess we'd best get to cleanin' the place up,' Ford suggested.

There was movement at the doorway and Kile appeared. He was alone.

Before Ford could speak, he said, 'I couldn't get you any help.'

'It's a good thing I found someone then, isn't it?'

Kile shifted his gaze to Potts who nodded at the storekeeper.

'What about me?'

All three men looked at the open doorway and saw a young woman standing there with red hair, green eyes, and pale skin. Gone was the dress, replaced by corduroy pants, a cotton shirt, high boots, and a low-crowned hat. What drew Ford's attention above all else was the single-action Colt in the holster on her shapely right thigh.

'You again,' Ford commented, dragging his eyes away from it.

'Small world, huh, marshal?' Eddie Yukon said, smiling.

'I already told you, Eddie, it's too dangerous for a . . . a . . . a woman,' Kile finally got out.

'Wait a minute,' Ford said. 'You know her?'

Kile nodded. 'Sheriff Frank Yukon was her brother. He was the first one killed by Cordis.'

Ford's gaze softened. 'I'm sorry about your brother, ma'am, but Mr Kile's right. It's too dangerous.'

'I can shoot as straight as any man here,' she stated adamantly.

'I've no doubt you probably can, but it doesn't change the fact that it's too dangerous.'

'There must be something I can do to help,' she offered.

Ford looked around the jail then back at Eddie. She realized what he was about to say and cut him off firmly with her raised hand. 'Uh-uh. No way. I'm not cleaning this place up. I don't clean.'

'If you want to help, it's all I have.'

'You know I come from . . '

'Yeah, I know,' Ford interrupted. 'You come from Deadwood. Tell me, what is it that you actually did in Deadwood?'

'I owned a saloon called the Yukon Belle,' she said proudly.

Ford frowned, thinking. He'd heard the name before . . . Then realization dawned on him. 'You're that Eddie Yukon?'

'Yes, I'm that Eddie Yukon,' she said. There was no boast in her voice, just a statement of fact.

Rumour had it that Eddie Yukon had stood beside Chris Tyler, the sheriff of Deadwood at that time, against a bunch of rioting miners. A drunken miner had tried to kill the sheriff who was then forced to put him down in self-defence. This event caused the riot because his fellow miners did not see it that way. With a head of courage fuelled by alcohol, they attempted to storm the jail.

Five miners died in a hail of lead that night before they finally gave up. Tyler was wounded and word was that Eddie Yukon had seen them off at the last. The funny thing was, Ford had always thought that Eddie Yukon was a man.

'All right,' Ford said in an authoritative voice. 'If you want to help, you clean up the jail.'

Eddie opened her mouth to protest again but Ford held up his hand and stopped her.

'After which,' he continued, 'we'll talk some more about what you can do that won't get you killed on day one.'

Eddie Yukon nodded. 'OK, we'll do it that way.'

'Now, hold on a minute,' Kile protested. 'You can't put her in danger like that. I won't allow it.'

Ford glowered at the storekeeper. 'Mr Kile, in case you've forgotten, apart from Potts, she was the only one in this lily-livered town who is willin' to stand up and be counted.'

Kile hung his head with the knowledge that Ford spoke the truth.

'Do you have a gunsmith in town?'

The storekeeper looked up at him and frowned. 'Yes, why?'

A pointed finger explained everything. 'Take Potts with you and get me some guns. Potts?'

'Yeah?'

'Get three messenger guns. If the gunsmith ain't got enough, have him cut them down,' Ford ordered. 'Get six boxes of shells to go with them. Also, I want three

Winchesters and another three Colts. Get ammunition for them too.'

'Wait a minute, who's paying for all of this?' Kile asked, tentatively.

'The town,' Ford said. 'Make it happen. I figure it's the least they can do if we're goin' to be layin' down our lives for them. I want the blacksmith too. We need to change the locks on the cells and have new keys made.'

Kile nodded silently.

Ford walked across to the battered desk, opened the top drawer and rummaged through its contents until he found what he wanted. He tossed it to Potts, who caught it before opening his hand to see what it was. A small, nickel-plated deputy sheriff's badge lay in his palm.

'Pin it on and let's go to work,' Ford told him.

The day progressed quite smoothly until the point that the fliers began to go up. Once brought to the attention of Ike Cordis, the prospect of losing money was not something he was willing to tolerate.

'Have you seen this?' Mort Bale asked as he placed the flier down on the table in front of Cordis.

Mort Bale was the manager of the small but profitable Ike's Place. It was a saloon but specialized more as a gambling establishment than the others. Its bar was shorter and the building was only single storey, compared to the others that all had two floors.

After reading it, Cordis looked at Bale. 'Well, well. If that didn't just make our new lawman the most unpopular person in town.'

'I should tell you that he's hired himself a deputy too,' Bale told him. 'The feller that give me that, said the

54

deputy was the one puttin' them up.'

'I see.' Cordis frowned. This was getting out of hand. It was about time he met their new peace officer and set a few things straight. 'Send word to the others that I want to see them.'

'Sure thing, boss,' Bale said and hurried away.

Ike Cordis sat pondering his next move. Should he get Beck to kill this one too? No. Perhaps a friendly discussion might suffice – let him know how things sit. If that didn't work, he might need to be persuaded. Or he would be killed.

Four people entered the jail as Ford placed the last messenger gun into the rack on the plank wall. Potts had returned earlier and was with Eddie out back in the cells, cleaning and preparing them for customers. Outside, the sun had dropped below the horizon and the jail was lit by the false orange glow from the desk lamp.

The approach of footsteps on floorboards made Ford turn around. Four people had gathered just inside the doorway; three of them were men. The fourth was a woman he knew. A woman he'd once loved. A woman who'd shot him.

'Hello Camilla,' Ford greeted her. 'It's been a while.'

The expression on her face was difficult for Ford to place. It was a combination of the first glimpse of a long-lost love and one loathing the man who'd killed her brother.

'Hello Josh,' she said drily. 'Still causing trouble everywhere you go, I see.'

Ford shrugged. 'Comes with the territory, I guess.'

Clearing his throat, Cordis interrupted. 'I see you two

know each other.'

'We go back aways,' Camilla acknowledged.

'Yeah, she shot me.'

'You killed my brother!' Camilla shot back.

'The son of a bitch was a murderer,' Ford barked. 'He got what he deserved.'

'And so did you,' Camilla snapped. 'Almost. Maybe this time you will.'

'This has started well,' Cordis said, sarcasm evident in his voice.

'Love what you've done with the place.'

'Who the hell are you?' Ford snapped, his eyes flaring. 'Although I have a fair idea.'

'I'm Ike Cordis,' Cordis informed Ford. 'These gentlemen are Justus Harper and Isom Friend. And seeing that Camilla needs no introduction, shall we get to the point of our visit?'

'Please.'

'We wanted to have a word with you, if that's all right?'

'What about?'

'Well, it seems to me that you've been sent here with the sole purpose of bringing law and order to Serenity. Am I right?'

'Listen, cut the horse crap and get to the point, Cordis. I like plain speakin' and I'm sure you're the same.'

A hint of color touched the outlaw boss' cheeks. 'OK, then. Here it is. You're here to clean up this town. That isn't going to happen without our cooperation. And you certainly won't get that, expecting the saloons to close at midnight every night. You, my friend, are going to cost me . . . us . . . a lot of money.'

'Let's get one thing straight, Cordis. I ain't your friend.

56

In fact, from what I've heard, you're lucky you ain't swingin' rope about now. But that will more than likely change before this is done.'

'You're a fool,' Cordis snarled. 'You can't beat us. The best you can hope for is a six-foot hole in the ground if you stay. But I'm willing to give you an amnesty of one day to make up your mind. After that, if you're still here, all bets are off.'

'Are you threatenin' me, Cordis?' Ford asked. 'Last time I looked, you were one gun down.'

Justus Harper stepped forward. 'Watch your step, lawman, I can turn upwards of a hundred men loose on this town and have it torn apart around you.'

Harper stepped closer to Ford and poked at the badge on his chest. 'Don't you forget it.'

Then Ford punched the bullish mine boss in the mouth.

CHAPTER 6

A meaty thwack sounded in the enclosed space as hard knuckles mashed against the lips of the mine boss. They split, bringing forth a rush of blood. Small rivulets began to flow freely down his chin and Harper staggered back but refused to go down. He shook his head to clear the cobwebs from the first blow and then let out a clamorous roar and charged.

Powerful arms locked around Ford, and Harper's momentum, with their combined weight, drove him backward against the wall between the office and cells with a bone-jarring crunch. Air gushed from Ford's lungs and his knees buckled slightly.

With his arms pinned to his side, Ford was helpless. The mine boss' grip tightened as he tried to crush the life from the deputy. Ford felt his ribs start to move from the extreme pressure and knew that Harper would likely kill him if he couldn't free himself.

The mine boss' eyes flashed wildly with glee. In a desperate attempt to break out, Ford brought his head forward with force in a crushing blow to the bridge of Harper's nose.

Blood sprayed from the ruined snout and Harper screamed with pain. His grip loosened and Ford pulled away then brought up a bunched fist and drove it at the center of Harper's face. Ford's arm jarred up to his shoulder from the impact. Once more the blow staggered Harper and he was forced to gather himself before he could consider another attack.

Blood cascaded from his mashed face and into his open mouth. It continued to run over his chin then dripped on to the floor.

'I'b goig' to kill you,' he said, blood spraying from his lips in small droplets.

The mine boss came forward, fists bunched. He swung at Ford's head with a powerful blow that would've ended the fight had it connected. As luck would have it, the fist glanced off the side of Ford's head.

Bright lights flashed in his eyes, and a fog of pain threatened to overwhelm him. This time, Ford backed away to escape further punishment, but Harper followed him. More blows rained down and Ford tasted blood in his mouth from one that mashed his lips against his teeth. Another made his left ear ring.

Ford was knocked sideways into the timber desk, causing it to move half a foot; its rounded edge drove into his ribs brutally, making him gasp. Ford regained his balance and straightened up ready to meet the next onslaught. It didn't take long, and a looping right skidded from the top of his shoulder and cracked against his jaw.

Ford managed to land one of his own. It was a solid punch that hit Harper just above his heart and stopped the advancing man in his tracks.

His mouth dropped open as he gasped for air. Ford

closed in again and drove two savage blows into his face. The first rocked Harper back on his heels, the second turned the lights out for the mine boss who fell like a tree in the forest. He hit the jail floor with a jarring thud and lay still.

Ford looked around the room as he took in great gulps of air. Eddie and Potts stood watching from the doorway that led through to the cells. Potts had his six-gun in his hand.

'Thanks for all your help,' Ford directed at Potts.

'No worries at all, pard',' Potts grinned. 'You seemed to have it all under control.'

Next, his gaze settled on Cordis.

'Take this pile of trash and get the hell out of my office,' Ford panted.

'You have one day, Ford,' Cordis snapped. 'Remember that. One day.'

Cordis and Friend managed to get the mine boss to his feet and out the door. Camilla stood staring at him, a sorrowful look in her eyes.

'You should leave before it's too late, Josh,' she advised him.

'Why do you care, Cam?' he asked, using his old name for her. 'After all, I killed your brother.'

For a moment her expression softened, then just as quick, it was gone, replaced by one that might be classed as pain.

'If you stay he'll kill you, Josh. Please go.'

He shook his head. 'I'm stayin', Cam. Maybe it should be you who leaves.'

Her shoulders fell and she turned and left. When she walked outside she literally ran into Cordis. He grabbed her arm in a cruel grip causing her face to contort with fear.

'How touching,' he whispered harshly. 'Let's get one thing straight. You belong to me now. There is no backing out. If you try to leave Serenity, I'll send Sam after you and have him drag you back by your hair. Now, get back to your whores!'

'What's next?' Potts asked Ford after Camilla had gone.

'We do what we can to enforce the law,' Ford said, answering his question. 'Once he realizes that we're here to stay, then he'll come at us.'

'I got me a feelin' that this town is about to live up to its name,' Potts said hesitantly.

'What, Serenity?' Eddie asked.

'No, Hell.'

The chill in the air that blew down from the high peaks of the Absarokas enveloped Serenity that evening. The boardwalks were dimly lit by lanterns and lamps, and long shadows reached out across the street and intersected with those from the opposite direction.

Somewhere around 10 o'clock, Ford and Potts were patrolling the town together when events turned decidedly worse.

Gunshots erupted from the Pink Garter followed quickly by the screams of a whore. It took only moments for both Ford and Potts to arrive and they pushed in through the batwings. The crowd of patrons were standing with their backs to the entrance and no one saw the two lawmen enter.

'Stay back or I'll shoot again,' a frightened voice said. 'I mean it, I'll shoot.'

'Let's get the murderin' son of a bitch, men,' another voice said. 'We'll string him up.'

Ford's voice cut through the smoke-filled room. 'Nobody's stringin' anybody up.'

Heads turned.

'Cover me,' he said to Potts out of the corner of his mouth and walked forward.

He pushed through the crowd and found a man dressed in a suit, holding a small gun in his shaking right hand. At his feet was a big man with two bullet holes in the chest. Beside the body's outstretched right hand lay a knife.

'He – he tried to kill me, marshal,' the man stammered. 'He was going to stick me with that knife.'

Frank Tulsa, the Pink Garter's manager, stepped forward. 'Lyle didn't mean no harm. He was just funning with him. There was no call to shoot him down cold like Harris did.'

Ford ignored the man and looked around the gathered crowd until he found another towner. 'Is that the way it was?'

The man paled and looked about, shrinking under the stares he was receiving. He opened and closed his mouth like a fish until he squeaked, 'I didn't see nothin.'

'Uh-huh,' Ford nodded.

His gaze shifted and settled on a large cowhand. 'How about you?'

'If I was Harris I woulda shot the son of a bitch too,' he said, causing a ripple of murmurs to spread through the crowd. 'Lyle was always doin' it for kicks. I always swore that if he tried it on me I'd kill him. Guess Harris beat me to it.'

'Why don't you shut your mouth, Grant,' a voice from the crowd said. 'Or we'll shut it for you.'

The big cowhand dropped his hand to his six-gun. He fixed his steely gaze on the speaker and spoke one word in a menacing tone, 'Anytime.'

'There'll be no more killin',' Ford snapped. He stepped towards Harris and held out his left hand. 'Give me the gun.'

An alarmed expression crossed the frightened man's face. 'Why? So you can take me in? It was self-defence.'

'Would you rather I leave you here?'

Harris hesitated for a moment longer then passed the weapon over.

'Now, go with Potts.'

Ford watched them leave and turned to face Tulsa. The rotund man had a look of disdain on his face.

'Remember, you close at midnight,' Ford said.

'And what if I don't?' Tulsa asked defiantly, hands on fleshy hips.

Ford moved in close to the saloon manager, making him shift nervously.

'If you don't, I'll come back here and tear the place down around your ears.'

Ford didn't wait for a response. He turned on his heel and stalked out of the saloon.

When he reached the jail, he found Potts and Harris in the main room. He put Harris' small gun in the top drawer then grabbed up the new set of keys left there by the blacksmith.

'Through that door, Mr Harris,' Ford directed him.

'You can't be serious, Marshal,' he blurted out. 'He would have killed me.'

'Do we have to lock him up, Josh?' Potts asked.

'How long do you think he'll last out there if we let him go?'

Potts shrugged.

'We lock him up for his own safety, for the time bein' anyway.'

'OK.'

'Now, wait a minute, you can't,' Harris protested.

But Ford ignored him. He was too busy trying to think what Cordis' next move would be.

The answer came soon after midnight when a crowd began to march along Absaroka Street, shouting and yelling, a rolling tidal wave of emotion. Some carried lanterns and most of them were armed. Their leader, a large, bullish man, carried a rope with a noose tied at the end of it.

After Ford's departure, Tulsa had gone to Ike Cordis, who demanded that every man be plied with as much free liquor as they could stand. Amongst the crowd were men sowing discontent, stirring them into frenzy. The result was the angry lynch mob that now approached the jail.

It didn't concern Cordis that there was the distinct possibility of shooting. In fact, he was counting on it. The outcome could solve all of his problems, providing Ford was killed of course.

Unaware of the mob's approach, Ford and Potts were drinking coffee when the jail door opened. Instinctively Ford's hand dropped to his Peacemaker but his draw was stayed by the appearance of Eddie Yukon as she entered the room.

'You are about to have a very big problem,' she said

urgently. 'Cordis stirred up the miners and the railway-men. They're all liquored to the eyeballs and comin' this way.'

There was no hurry to Ford's movements as he stood up. He walked over to the gun rack and took down a messenger gun. He checked to see if it was loaded, then walked towards the door.

'You'd best grab yourselves one of these if you figure to follow me,' he called back over his shoulder. 'I think it might get a little heated on the street.'

By the time they walked outside, Ford was in the middle of the shadow-shrouded street awaiting the mob's arrival. Potts took his left while Eddie stood to his right.

'You don't have to do this,' he said to her out of the corner of his mouth.

'They killed my brother. I'm not walking away now.'

'OK. Potts, move across to the boardwalk on the other side of the street. Keep to the shadows. Eddie, you do this side. Again, stay in the shadows.'

They both did as he ordered then settled in the darkness to wait.

It wasn't long before one of the approaching crowd shouted, 'There the son of a bitch is!'

The crowd was fifteen feet from him when Ford called out, 'That's far enough. Go away and sleep it off.'

'The hell we will,' roared a big slab of a man who raised up the rope they intended to use. 'That bastard in there killed my friend, and he's goin' to swing for it.'

'I'm sorry about your friend,' Ford said, trying to defuse the situation, 'but if you threaten another man with a knife, well, you can expect a slug in the guts.'

'What are you goin' to do about him, marshal?' another

65

man called out.

'I'll investigate the matter and go from there. If it's self-defence, then I'll let him go.'

'C'mon fellers, let's string the son of a bitch up,' another man shouted. 'The law ain't goin' to do nothin' about it.'

The crowd roared their approval at the suggestion and they started to move forward as one. Ford brought the messenger gun level and thumbed back both hammers.

'If any of you keep comin', I'm goin' to unload a world of pain on you all. This is a job for the law, not some rabble like you lot. You'll not be havin' a neck-tie party while I'm around.'

'That suits me just fine,' the rope carrier said, and moved forward in a threatening manner.

Ford let loose with one barrel of the messenger gun, its throaty roar reverberating from the false-fronts along the street. The rope holder went down, shot below the right knee, his high-pitched scream replacing the echo of the shot. He rolled around grasping at the shattered appendage.

The crowd was stunned into silence by the sheer violence of the act and some stepped back when the messenger gun came up and pointed directly at them.

A sudden shout from Potts split the silence. 'On the roof!'

As Ford began to move, the thunder from Potts' shotgun rolled down the street. A cry of pain sounded and the bushwhacker pitched forward off the roof.

'There's one on the other side!' Eddie screeched.

The shadows of her hiding spot came to life with a bright flash of flame from the gun muzzles. The sound of a shot reverberated once more and its echo almost drowned out the pain-filled howl.

Ford had dived and rolled to throw off the ambushers' aim and now came up to his knees. He glanced up at the rooflines, searching for further threats. Seeing they were clear, he returned his attention to the crowd. He stood up and walked towards them.

'You all have one minute to get off the street,' Ford ordered. 'And someone get this piece of trash to the doc before he bleeds to death.'

They hesitated.

'Move, damn it!'

Four men came forward and helped their now whimpering friend. The rest of them turned to leave.

'Wait!' Ford snapped.

When they stopped, he said, 'Don't forget the other two.'

Potts and Eddie came over to him and stood by his side.

'Thanks for savin' my skin,' Ford said to them.

'I got me a feelin' that we may be pullin' your chestnuts from the fire a few more times before this is done,' Potts said.

'I got a feelin' you could be right.'

CHAPTER 7

In the back room of the Royal Palace, Ike Cordis fumed as he stalked back and forth across his office. The situation was getting out of control and he was ready for it to go away. The affair was costing him men and money. And he hated to lose money.

He threw back his fourth glass of whiskey and slammed the empty vessel down on the polished woodwork of his desk.

'Enough is enough,' he hissed menacingly. 'This is my town and I want that bastard gone.'

'Say the word,' Sam Beck said to his boss.

'No. Not you. The last thing I want is for my top gun to be wanted by federal marshals. Get Raven. Have him do it.'

Beck nodded. 'OK. I'll get on to it.'

'Who the hell does this son of a bitch think he is?' Cordis snarled.

'He's the Fourth Horseman,' Camilla giggled.

Cordis glared at her. 'What?'

'Oh, come on, Ike,' Camilla said to him. 'You know what

I'm saying. The whole Fourth Horseman thing. Except he ain't riding a white horse. But his name, sure enough, is Death.'

Cordis snorted derisively. 'I think you rate him a little too highly.'

'We'll see.'

He waved a dismissive hand at her and turned back to Beck. 'Have you found out who sent word, yet?'

Beck shook his head. 'Nope. It won't be long, though.'

'Hurry it up. I want things back to normal.'

After Beck was gone, Cordis turned to Camilla. 'What is it between you and this Ford?'

'What do you mean?'

'You know what I mean.'

'He killed my brother.'

'Not that, damn it,' Cordis flared. 'The other thing between you and him. What?'

'We had – we were lovers. OK? Right up until my brother robbed a stage carrying a mail consignment and $5,000 in gold.'

'And?'

'When he tracked down the outlaws who did it, my brother was among them,' Camilla went on. 'He thought he was better than Ford. He was wrong and paid for it with a bullet. When Josh told me about it I was so mad, I shot him. It was done before I'd even realized that I had pulled the trigger. That was four years ago.'

'So why didn't they put you in prison?'

'I don't know. I ran and kept running. But after a while, I'd heard nothing about it, so I settled down and looked for work. And that's when you found me.'

'That's right,' Cordis snapped. '*I* found you. *I* made you

69

what you are today. Just you remember that. You belong to me.'

'I belong to no one,' Camilla hissed back at him.

With blinding speed, Cordis reached out and dragged her close. 'You . . . belong . . . to . . . *me.*'

The defiant look in Camilla's eyes was backed by the dry triple-click of a gun hammer going back and the firm press of a cold gun barrel against the underside of Cordis' chin.

'Let me go, Ike,' she said in a menacing tone. 'They may call you 'The Devil', but you can die just like any other man.'

Without changing expression, Cordis released her arm. Camilla took a step back but left the gun trained on the outlaw. 'Let this be your first and final warning, Ike. If you ever do that again, I won't hesitate to pull the trigger.'

'You just stay away from him.'

Camilla snorted contemptuously. 'You go to hell, Ike.'

He watched her leave and when the door closed behind her he said, 'I'm already there.'

The Rocking K ranch drew its water from the Rocky Bottom Creek, and its owner, William Krouse, was far from happy when he hit town the following morning. He flung the jail door open and strode in purposefully and came to stand in front of Ford's desk. He said in an angry voice, 'What are you goin' to do about it?'

Ford looked up into the lined face of a tall, grey-headed man. 'About what exactly, Mr. . . ?'

'Krouse, William Krouse. I'm the owner of the Rocking K,' the ranch owner said.

'OK. Mr Krouse, what exactly is it that you want me to do?'

'I want you to shut down that damned mine, marshal, is what I want you to do,' Krouse grumbled. 'The bastards are poisonin' the creek and killin' my stock. When I heard that there was a marshal in town, I thought maybe somethin' could be done about it.'

'How long has this been goin' on?' Ford asked.

'About a month.'

'Why hasn't somethin' been done about it already?'

'The previous sheriff tried and all they did was laugh at him,' Krouse explained.

'I see.'

When Ford didn't move, Krouse snapped. 'Are you goin' to do something' about it or what?'

Ford nodded. 'I'll come out and have a look around. Just give me twenty or so minutes to get my horse and I'll be with you.'

The reply seemed to placate the rancher and his animosity vanished. 'That would be great. Thanks.'

'Potts?' Ford called out. 'Are you back there?'

The deputy put his head through the door that led to the jail cells. 'Yeah.'

'I'm goin' outta town with Mr Krouse,' Ford informed him. 'You're in charge. 'If you have any problems, make a decision and act on it. Don't hesitate. If it means shootin' someone, then so be it.'

'What about our prisoner back here?' Potts asked.

'I'll see to him when I get back.'

Ford turned back to the rancher. 'All right, Mr Krouse. I'll get my horse and be right with you.'

Krouse nodded. 'You know, when I heard about a new lawman in Serenity, I was more than a little sceptical. Now, maybe I ain't too sure.'

'Save your judgement for after, Mr Krouse,' Ford said to him.

'After what?'

'After I clean the town up and give it back to the people. C'mon, let's go.'

The Rocking K was in the lea of a large craggy-faced, snow-covered peak that watched over it as a father would a child. Through the tree-lined landscape of lush pasture and rolling hills, ran the Rocky Bottom creek. What had once been a clear, pristine waterway, was now a stinking, slimy, green sludge that bore no resemblance to its former self, and Ford looked down upon it from beside the ranch owner.

'See what I mean?' Krouse said, his hand covering his mouth.

And he did see. Out in the middle of the creek lay the bloated carcass of a once prime beast. It wasn't the only one either. Another two lay on the far bank, and countless fish floated past on the current. The smell that emanated from the creek was one of putrefaction from the decaying beasts, combined with that of the sludge, and was overwhelmingly stomach turning.

'I had to shift all of my cattle over on to a neighbor's range to get them away from this water,' Krouse told Ford. 'I was just lucky that he had plenty of water.'

Ford spat on the ground, trying to rid his mouth of the taste left by the smell. He walked back over to his blue roan and climbed into the saddle. The sound of a powder blast trying to escape the valley rolled along the tops of the peaks.

'What are you goin' to do?' Krouse asked, for the tenth time.

'I'm goin' to shut them down,' Ford told him.

'Do you want some help?'

'Nope. I can handle it.'

'Watch your back over there,' Krouse warned.

'Always do,' said Ford as he swung the head of his roan around and pointed it towards the mine.

It was a brutal, ugly, man-made scar upon what had once been untouched wilderness. The land had been dug up by men, greedy for what lay beneath the surface, and their tool of extraction was hydraulic mining.

Ford had seen it all before. Big companies moved in, took what they wanted, and then abandoned the site, leaving naught but a wounded and barren landscape. Good for nothing.

Miners stared at Ford as he rode on to the mine site. He stopped the roan near a couple of them and asked, 'Where's Harper?'

The miner looked him over before answering. 'He's over at the tent.'

Ford looked up and saw four stained canvas tents sitting in the centre of a piece of level ground.

'Which one?'

'The big one.'

'Thanks,' Ford said and turned the roan towards the tent area.

When he reached them, Ford climbed down from the horse. He flipped the rawhide hammer-thong off and walked inside the largest tent. He found Harper sitting behind a large desk going over surveyor's maps.

The man looked up and Ford saw evidence of their fight still obvious on his face. When he saw who it was, he screwed up his face in a snarl. 'What the hell do you want?'

'Have you seen the mess your hydraulic mining is makin' of the creek? It's ruinin' all the water for the ranchers downstream.'

'So what?'

'So, get it cleaned up,' Ford ordered. 'Until then, you're shut down.'

'The hell you say,' Harper exploded.

'The hell I do. You shut it down or I'll do it for you.'

Harper roared and lurched from his desk, clawing at the six-gun on his hip. Ford's Peacemaker was out in a flash and aimed at the mine boss' heart. His jaw dropped.

'Don't,' Ford snapped. 'I'll kill you where you stand.'

Harper froze, his face white as he waited for the shot that would end his life.

'Drop it,' Ford ordered.

Harper tossed it on his desk. 'Now what?'

'You're a lucky man, Harper. I would have killed most men by now but I'll give you a chance.'

'Why?'

'Because you're goin' to shut this mine down and order all your men from site,' Ford explained. 'After which, I'm goin' back to town and I'll wire your boss and tell him why I've closed down his mine.'

'You can't do that,' Harper blurted out. 'He'll fire me.'

'Better that than dead,' Ford allowed. He waved the Colt. 'Let's go.'

The mine boss moved from behind the desk and walked out into the brilliant sunshine. He looked about until he saw the man he was looking for. He called out and a large mountain of a man ambled over to him. He saw the gun in Ford's fist and started.

74

'What the hell is goin' on here?' his baritone voice rumbled.

'Shut the mine down, Jeff and get all the men off the site,' Harper told him hesitantly.

'Say what?'

'Are you deaf or somethin'? Harper snapped. 'Shut it down.'

Jeff glanced at Ford then back at Harper. 'Are you sure?'

'Damn it, Jeff!' barked Harper. 'Just bloody well do it.'

The big man lumbered off and Harper turned to face Ford. 'Are you happy?'

'I'll be happy when all you bastards are run out of Serenity,' Ford cursed. 'But for now, this'll do. If I find out that you have resumed operations before the problem is rectified, I will come back out here, take some of your black powder and blow it all to hell.'

Harper stared at him in a display of open defiance.

'And one more thing,' Ford said, stepping towards the mine boss.

The butt of the Peacemaker came up and Ford slammed it into the middle of the man's already bruised face.

'That's for tryin' to pull a gun on me. Next time you'll get the bullet end.'

CHAPTER 8

'The son of a bitch shut the mine down, just like that,' Harper whined. 'Just like that!'

'I'll have a word to the judge,' Cordis told the irate mine boss. 'He'll see things our way.'

'Do you think?' Harper asked, hopefully.

'I'm sure,' Cordis replied. 'Anyway, don't worry about that at the moment, it all might be a moot point.'

'How so?'

'Let's just say I have someone taking care of it, tonight.'

'I sure hope so,' Isom Friend put in. 'Without the miners, the profits in town are goin' to take a big hit.'

Cordis nodded in agreement and said, 'Get all of your boys in town tonight. I want as much going on as possible so our new lawman will be required out on the street to keep an eye on things. He'll present more of a target that way.'

Both men agreed to the request.

'Just make sure your man don't miss,' Friend warned. 'I got me a feelin' that this feller will only take so much before he releases his own brand of hell upon the town.'

'The town sure is jumpin' tonight,' Potts said, on entering the jail.

'Yeah,' Ford allowed. 'Maybe a little too high.'

Ford had noticed the change just before sunset. Men had flooded into Serenity and things started to get loud from then on. Now, at around 9 o'clock, things were, as Potts had said, jumping.

Ford's deputy caught the worried expression on his face and asked, 'Are you worried that Cordis is up to somethin'?'

Ford nodded. 'He's up to somethin', all right. Blowed if I know what, though.'

Potts walked over to the gun rack and took down two of the messenger guns. He handed one across to Ford and said, 'Shall we go find out?'

'It's probably what he wants.' Ford pointed out.

'No one lives forever,' Potts said dismissively.

'I wouldn't mind tryin'.'

The sound of gunshots filled the night.

'Sounds like somebody cuttin' loose,' Potts said.

'Yeah, c'mon then, let's go.'

Outside, the noise was louder. It pervaded the cool night air and drifted all along Absaroka Street.

'Where do you want to start?' Potts asked.

'We'll stroll along this side and check things out,' Ford told him. 'After we reach the end we'll come back and check out the back streets. Keep on your toes.'

As they passed each of the four saloons, Ford put his head inside to look around. Their rounds suffered a short interruption when they had to lock a drunk away. With that done, they continued their task.

From the shadows, their progress was being constantly

tracked. The bushwhacker, Raven Morris, waited patiently for what he considered the right time, then cut loose from the cover of a darkened alley.

Ford felt the slug pass close to his face. A second gunshot came followed by a grunt from Potts as the bullet buried into his chest. Ford glanced sideways and saw Potts start to buckle at the knees.

'Potts,' he called out in alarm.

'I'm OK,' the deputy groaned and kept falling.

Another shot rang out and the window behind Ford shattered. He brought the messenger gun into action. It bucked hard in the deputy marshal's hands, sending its deadly load scything into the shadows across the street. He cast it aside and drew his Peacemaker. Without thought for his own safety, Ford advanced out on to the street, a measured rate of fire for a few shots aimed at the bushwhacker's position.

A slug burned the air as it whipped past, leaving behind the pungent smell of cordite, as it disappeared into the night. Ford fired his fifth shot as he moved forward, which forced the bushwhacker to break cover. He'd been hiding behind a water barrel that had begun to leak profusely.

The last shot from the Peacemaker cracked and the man staggered, went down on one knee, but got up to run again, this time with a pronounced limp.

While Ford was reloading the Colt, Eddie appeared. 'What happened?'

'We got bushwhacked,' Ford told her without looking up. 'Check on Potts.'

While she did, Ford picked up his messenger gun and stuffed the breech with fresh loads. There was movement at his side and Eddie spoke quietly. 'He's dead.'

Ford cursed under his breath.

'I knew there was a reason for all of this noise,' Ford told her. 'Now I know why. It was to lure us out so that someone could take a shot at me.'

'How do you know it was just you?'

'It ain't hard to work out.'

'Where did he go?'

'The Dead Dog,' Ford told her. 'I saw him go in through the doors. He's bleedin', though. I managed to put a slug in his leg. Pity it wasn't his brain, it would have made my next job easier.'

'Surely, you're not...?' her voice trailed away, but concern showed on her face.

'Someone has to,' Ford said. 'He killed a duly appointed lawman.'

'Yes, but look where he is.'

'I'll be fine,' he tried to sound convincing.

'At least let me help,' Eddie suggested.

He considered saying no but the simple fact was he needed her. 'All right. I want you to stand outside the saloon with Potts' messenger gun. You stop anyone from enterin'. The last thing I need is someone comin' at me from behind with a six-gun and puttin' a slug in my back.'

Eddie readily agreed and retrieved the dead deputy's shotgun.

'Now remember, whatever happens, don't come in,' Ford warned her. 'If I get killed, then leave town. Find United States Marshal Bass Reeves and tell him what happened.'

Eddie hesitated before saying, 'OK.'

'Right, then let's go and find ourselves a killer.'

They walked along Absaroka Street with shotguns

loaded and ready. Once level with the saloon, Ford paused, then thumbed back both hammers and trod calmly towards the boardwalk. He stepped up on to the warped planks and hurried across to the doors, Eddie a short distance behind him ready to take up her post.

As he was about to push through, a man emerged from inside. Ford brought the butt of the gun up in a sharp arc under the man's chin. A couple of his teeth shattered from the impact and he reeled backward into the saloon. Ford followed close behind and before anyone could react, he unloaded one of the messenger gun's barrels into the ceiling.

'Listen up!' he shouted and waited for the raucous noise to abate. 'A few minutes ago, a man limped in here. I say limped because I shot him.'

A murmur rippled through the crowd.

'No one came in here,' a large miner snapped. 'Get outta here before you're carried out.'

Ford approached the man and stopped in front of him. He was a full head taller than the deputy marshal but Ford didn't let that intimidate him.

'There's a blood trail on the floor, friend. Are you still sayin' that nobody came in here?'

'Damn right.'

'And if I tell you that this man just shot and killed my deputy?'

A brazen smile split the man's face. 'Too bad.'

The butt of the messenger gun travelled the short distance between them and slammed into the man's gut with brutal force. He doubled over, gasping for breath, and Ford followed up by bringing the gun crashing down on the base of his skull, turning his lights out.

Ford looked up at the gathered crowd through the haze of the smoke-filled room. There was uncertainty on many faces but an element of defiance on others.

'Like I was sayin', I'm after a feller who came in here.'

'No one came in here! Are you deaf or somethin'?'

Ford watched as the crowd parted and let Cordis and Sam Beck through.

'So I keep gettin' told,' Ford responded. 'But that blood trail on the floor there tells me different. It seems to go on over to the bar.'

'Had a drunk rail worker in here earlier,' Cordis explained. 'Fell and cut himself on the glass he was carry-ing. Nasty wound.'

Ford glanced about the room and his attention was drawn to a man on the landing at the top of the stairs a Winchester in his hands. The position gave him a clear shot at Ford who assumed that the man would fire on Cordis' say so.

Ford nodded, apparently accepting the explanation. Instead, he changed the shotgun to his left hand to free up his right. Then he pointed the weapon at the crowd in front of himself and said, 'Move.'

No man, drunk or sober, wanted to argue with a loaded messenger gun. Some had already seen what it would do and knew that Ford wasn't afraid to use it.

With cautious moves, they stepped back, clearing a path between Ford and the bar. He never moved. He called out, 'I know you're behind the bar. I can see the blood trail leadin' straight to it!'

The bartender paled and darted out of the way.

A heavy silence hung in the air.

'Come on out,' Ford called again.

When nothing happened, Beck sneered, 'Looks like you were mistaken, marshal. Ain't nobody come in here, so how about you haul your freight back outside.'

Ford showed no annoyance at the smug look on Beck's face. Then the deputy marshal did the last thing they expected.

He squeezed the trigger.

CHAPTER 9

Thunder from the messenger gun filled the room as flame and smoke belched from its cut-down barrel. Most of the buckshot charge shattered the long mirror that hung on the wall behind the bar, smashing bottles on the shelves in front of it.

Sharp shards of glass and wooden splinters rained down behind the bar bringing forth a yelp of fear and pain. The concealed man leaped up covered in glass and alcohol. He brought up his six-gun to fire at Ford, but the deputy marshal had his Peacemaker out and fired.

It bucked in his fist and the man spun around from the bullet strike. With a loud cry of pain, he fell to the floor. Ford swiveled at the hip and lifted the angle of his Peacemaker. The foresight settled on the gunman on the landing, who was in the process of sighting his rifle on Ford's chest when the deputy marshal fired again.

Two shots this time. Both took the would-be shooter in the chest, and he dropped his rifle and fell forward. He hit just below the top step and bumped and crashed down the stairs until he landed in a jumbled heap at the foot of them.

The Colt swung back to cover Beck and Cordis. 'You were sayin'?'

Both men remained silent.

'Eddie, are you still there?' Ford called over his shoulder.

'I'm here!'

'Step inside a moment, will you?'

When she entered the saloon, Eddie immediately moved to her left, keeping the wall at her back. She met a withering glare from Cordis with one of defiance.

'You need to leave,' the hotel owner told her in a caustic voice. 'This ain't got nothing to do with you.'

A cold smile split her lips. 'Can I shoot him, Josh?'

'Only if he needs it.'

'Oh, he needs it all right,' she said, raising the messenger gun.

'You know what I mean.'

Eddie's green eyes sparkled, 'Shame. I was looking forward to killing him.'

'Who the hell are you?' Cordis snarled.

'I'm Eddie Yukon. Remember the name for when I do kill you,' she sneered.

Recognition at the name crossed Cordis' face.

'That's right. My brother was the sheriff here until you bastards killed him.'

'If you're all done gettin' acquainted, would you mind keepin' an eye on them?' Ford broke in.

'With pleasure,' Eddie said.

Ford moved towards the bar. He walked behind it, glass from the mirror and bottles crunching beneath his boots. He bent down and dragged the wounded bushwhacker to his feet where he could get a look at him.

'Hello Raven,' Ford greeted him.

Raven moaned with the pain of his wounds.

'Looks like you'll have a date with the rope,' Ford told him.

Alarm flitted across Raven Morris' face and his eyes darted to Cordis. 'I ain't goin' to hang.'

'Shut up, Raven,' Cordis snapped.

'The hell with you,' Morris bleated. His eyes locked on Ford. 'OK. I'll tell you what you want to know. But you can't hang me.'

'Who put you up to it, Morris?' Ford asked him.

'It was . . '

The roar of a gunshot filled the room and Morris clutched at his chest. His face contorted with pain before it relaxed and the bushwhacker fell dead.

Ford clawed at his Peacemaker and had it cocked and aimed in an instant. His trigger-finger was stayed by the sight of Ike Cordis with his arms raised and a still-smoking six-gun in his right hand.

'Drop the gun!' Ford shouted at Cordis.

With a nonchalant expression on his face, Cordis shrugged and did as he was ordered. The gun thudded loudly on the timber floor.

'Son of a bitch,' Ford cursed. 'It looks like you'll take his place on the gallows. Turn around and start walkin'.'

'Where we going?' Cordis asked.

'Where do you think? Jail of course.'

Beck took a step forward to block their path. Ford sighted the Peacemaker on his chest.

'Get the hell out of the way, Beck,' Ford ordered. 'Or I'll blow you full of holes.'

'It's OK, Sam,' Cordis assured his man. 'I'm sure the

judge will have no hesitation in seeing that it was a case of self-defence.'

'Move, Cordis,' Ford said and followed the killer out the door with Eddie close behind.

When the door to the jail opened just after midnight, the last person Ford expected to see was Camilla. As usual, she looked lovely in a floor-length, red dress that was low cut to accentuate the swell of her breasts.

Just the sight of her took Ford's breath away. It didn't matter that she'd shot him; the old feelings were still there and he hated himself for feeling that way.

'What are you doin' here, Camilla?' Ford snapped at her.

She blanched at the vehemence of his words. She gathered herself and said, 'I came to warn you.'

'About what?'

'Isom Friend is gathering men to come and bust Ike out of jail.'

'Let them come,' Ford told her.

'They'll kill you, Josh,' she blurted out, her concern showing.

'No, they won't.'

Then she realized. This was the Josh Ford he'd always been. The man she'd loved and still did.

'You haven't changed,' she said coldly. 'Still have to do everything yourself no matter what. Even if it gets you killed.'

'Comes with the badge,' he said stoically.

'You're a damned fool.'

A wry smile touched his lips. 'You and Bass need to get together. I've heard this tune played before.'

Anger flushed her face. 'Damn you to hell, Josh Ford.'

'Maybe one day, but not today.'

'I hope they shoot you in your ass,' she hissed and stormed out.

'That woman still loves you,' Eddie said from the doorway.

'Did you hear what she said about Friend?'

'Yeah, I did. They don't let up, do they?'

'Maybe you should make yourself scarce,' Ford suggested.

'A smart girl would do just that,' Eddie agreed. 'But I never considered myself to be one of those. I reckon I might sit out the back there with a messenger gun. And if they break in here, then I might just unload that gun, straight at that son of a bitch you got locked up.'

'You don't have to do this,' Ford told her.

'He had my brother killed, so yeah, I do.'

Ford stared into her emerald-green eyes for a long moment before the growing noise outside broke the moment.

'You'd best get out the back,' Ford told her.

Eddie's gaze dropped briefly before she looked back up and nodded. 'You be careful.'

Ford grabbed a messenger gun from the rack. 'I always am.'

Out on the boardwalk in the dim lamp light, Ford could see the rowdy gathering rolling along Absaroka Street like a rising tide. They stopped in front of the jail and Isom Friend stepped forward.

'We've come for Ike,' he said in a brave voice. 'Let him out.'

'I would have thought that you lot would've learned

from the last time you pulled somethin' like this!' Ford shouted above the noisy crowd. 'This time someone will die if you try anythin'. You've been warned.'

Friend took another step forward. 'The hell they will.'

The night was rocked as the charge of buckshot exploded from the barrel of the messenger gun in Ford's hands. It smashed into Friend's chest and threw him backwards into the crowd.

A stunned silence replaced the echoes of the shot as the mob stared collectively down at the dead railway boss.

'Murderin' son of a bitch!' a man called out.

Ford shifted the aim of the messenger gun, and those in the front of the crowd cringed as they braced for the discharge of the second barrel.

'You've all got a choice to make,' Ford told them. 'Go home or join your *friend* here.'

A ripple of uncertainty ran through the crowd and, one by one, they began to disperse.

Ford stood watching them until the last one had disappeared, taking the limp form of Isom Friend away. Once again, quiet settled over the streets of Serenity, but Ford knew there would be worse to come. There always was.

The Serenity courthouse had once been the town church. However, once construction had been completed on the new church on the outskirts of town, the court was moved from one of the saloons to its current location.

Ford pushed Cordis down into a wooden chair at the desk utilized as the defendant's table. He looked around the surprisingly well-lit room at the people already seated, waiting for the trial to begin. Only a small few were townsfolk. The bulk was made up of miners and rail workers.

'Looks to be a good turnout,' Cordis commented. 'Eager for the judge's decision no doubt.'

'Shut it, Cordis,' Ford snapped. 'Let's see if you're smilin' when the judge puts a noose around your neck.'

'Yes, let's.' Cordis smiled back.

Within minutes of their arrival, the judge, a round man with flabby jowls and large, red, bulbous nose, entered and stood behind his desk. The court clerk was about to speak but was cut short by the overweight man's impatient voice. 'Having reviewed the case and looked at the evidence, or rather lack of it, I feel that this matter going forward would be a waste of more than just my time.'

'Your honour,' Ford said, confusion evident on his face.

'Therefore,' he proceeded, as though oblivious that anyone had spoken, 'I see no point in continuing. Case dismissed.'

There was uproar in the courtroom at the unexpected announcement. Ford looked at Cordis who sat there with a smug expression on his face.

The judge reached forward and picked up his gavel, its banging sounded like gunshots in the confined space.

'Order! Order! Quiet I say!' the judge roared.

After a moment, the noise died down but before the judge could speak again, Ford interrupted.

'I would like to know how you came to that conclusion, Judge,' Ford demanded.

'And you are?' he asked, as though becoming aware of Ford's presence for the first time.

'United States Marshal Josh Ford.'

'Ahh yes, the killer with a badge. You're lucky that you are not on trial.'

Ford ignored the remark and asked, 'How can you

dismiss the charges when he shot the man down in cold blood in front of a saloon full of witnesses?'

'What witnesses?' the judge asked. 'Do you see any in this courtroom?'

'I'm sorry, Judge, might I ask your name?'

'Why?'

'I need to fill out a report when I'm finished, and the marshal's office is a stickler for dottin' 'i's and crossin' 't's.'

'I see. Very well, my name is Lemuel Jackson.'

Ford's mind worked overtime as he tried to figure out if he'd heard the name before.

'Is there anything else?'

'Yes, why can't you take my testimony? After all, I was there,' Ford suggested, stalling.

Jackson frowned. 'I suppose we could do that, if you insist. But it would do no good because I've already dismissed the case.'

Ford remained silent. He knew his offer had been a waste of time but the few moments gained by the stall had been sufficient to trigger his memory.

'You know, I heard of a judge by the name of Jackson once,' Ford said aloud. 'He used to run a courtroom in St Louis. The word was he could be bribed with a bottle of rye. Anyway, he was caught out and ended up doin' a year in the pen.'

As Ford spoke he saw the man's face pale. 'You wouldn't be him by any chance, would you?'

'No, no. Most definitely not,' Jackson blustered and directed his gaze to Cordis. 'Mr Cordis. You're free to go.'

The deputy marshal looked at the prosecuting attorney. 'Are you just goin' to let this happen?'

The lawyer gave him a helpless look.

Ford shook his head and turned to leave when Jackson stopped him.

'There was one other thing,' the judge said.

Ford stopped to look at him.

'The mine is reopened and the miners can go back to work.'

A cheer echoed around the room.

'What about the creek?' Ford asked. 'The mine poisoned it.'

'I have assurances that it all will be fixed,' Jackson said.

Without looking back, Ford walked out the door. There was only one way to stop Cordis. With lead.

And little did he know, Hell was about to live up to its name.

CHAPTER 10

The reopening of the mine was cause for celebration, which is exactly what most did. With Ike Cordis fueling them with copious amounts of booze, the miners were cutting loose in the Dead Dog.

Ely, the saloon manager, approached the table where Cordis sat with Sam Beck, California Wells, Justus Harper, and Camilla. The latter began to look worried.

'It's time to close up,' Ely said to Cordis.

'Go away, Ely,' Harper slurred. 'Can't you see we're havin' us a celebration.'

'But the marshal. . . .'

'Who gives a crap about the marshal,' Harper snapped.

Ely looked at Cordis who nodded and waved him away.

'Are you sure this is wise, Ike?' Camilla asked Cordis. 'He ain't going to let this stand.'

'Our marshal has grown too big for his britches, my dear,' Cordis told her. 'He seems to need reminding who runs our town.'

'Maybe it's you who needs reminding,' Camilla said harshly. 'From where I'm sitting, you haven't been doing so well of late.'

Cordis' eyes grew cold. 'And maybe you need to be reminded of where you actually sit in all of this.'

Suddenly the room grew quiet and the crowd parted enough which allowed Cordis sufficient space to see the figure standing just inside the saloon entrance. He wore his hat pulled down low, his right hand held what was becoming his trademark. The sawn-off messenger gun. In his left hand, Ford held something long and cylindrical.

It took a moment for them to register what it was then someone gasped, 'Dynamite!'

Cautiously a few of the miners edged past Ford and vacated the premises. Others stood and stared, unsure whether the lawman was bluffing or meant what he was implying.

'This place is closed!' Ford's voice rang out. 'From now until I see fit to allow it to open.'

The last of his words were directed at Cordis.

'You ain't got the stones to do that in here, Ford,' Harper snapped in his drink-induced bravery.

'Try me.'

Harper gave a sharp nod. 'I'll pay any man here $2,000 to kill this pain in the ass.'

The offer brought forth a string of murmurs before a voice said, 'I'll take that contract.'

California Wells stood up from the table and moved to one side. The crowd backed away to give a clearer line of fire.

'This should be interesting,' Cordis mused. 'Wells ain't no two-bit hack with a gun.'

Ford placed the unlit stick of dynamite into his coat pocket and changed the messenger gun into his left hand. He let his right hand drop to the Peacemaker's butt and said to Harper, 'Think very carefully about your next answer. If he draws his gun on me I'm goin' to kill him and then you. Do you still want to walk that trail?'

'Hell, yes!' Harper shouted. 'Shoot the son of a bitch, Wells.'

Before the last words were out of his mouth, Ford had commenced his draw. It was a blur of movement that even the best fast-guns in the business would've been proud of. The colt came up level and a shot crashed out.

California Wells may not have been a 'two-bit hack', as Cordis had put it, but he wasn't in the class of Ford when it came to gun-speed. The slug punched into his chest, knocking him backward. A second shot hammered into him a short distance from the first, sealing his fate.

Ford shifted his aim and, without hesitation, made good on his word when the Peacemaker belched flame from its barrel and the bullet opened a neat hole in Harper's forehead. The mine boss jerked back with enough force for his chair to tip and he clattered to the floor.

The Peacemaker moved once more and settled on the chest of Ike Cordis. He was unmoved and his face remained passive.

Once more a gunshot rang out, only this time it was Ford who fell under the bullet strike. He went to his knees, air knocked from his lungs with the force. He opened his mouth to speak.

'You bitch. You shot me again.'

'Someone had to,' Camilla said. 'You needed it.'

The room spun and Ford fell flat on his face.

Cordis stood up from his seat, his fist filled with his own six-gun. He looked at Camilla and the still-smoking gun in her clenched hand.

'Saved me a bullet,' he said gruffly. 'Although, you were the last person I figured to put a slug in him.'

'Why?' she asked curtly. 'You seem to forget, I shot him once before when he killed my brother.'

Cordis stared at her for a long moment then looked down at the dead men on the floor. He shook his head in disgust and pointed at the miners nearest.

'Get them outta here,' he barked.

'And do what?' one of the men asked.

'I don't care,' Cordis said. 'Take them to the under-taker.'

A few minutes later, Ford was being dragged out by his feet, leaving a trail of blood behind him.

His whole body hurt like a bitch, especially his chest. That felt like his damned roan had kicked him there. He moved his arm and the action brought forth a low moan.

'You take it easy, honey,' a soft voice said. 'Or you'll start bleedin' again.'

Ford cracked his eyes open a touch and a pale face swam in front of him. He closed them again and waited a moment before trying once more. This time the face came into focus and he could put large brown eyes to it.

Her face was framed by black hair and her lips were full. She smiled and said, 'It's good to see you awake, hand-some. I ain't never had a man in my bed as long as you before. I was startin' to think maybe we'd got married and I'd not been told.'

'Water?' Ford asked, his voice gravelly and dry.

'Sure.'

The woman stood up from beside the bed and Ford got

a better look at her. She wore nothing but pantalets and a red corset that forced her milky-white breasts upward so that they almost billowed over the top. From behind he could see that her hair stopped halfway down her back.

She walked to a cupboard against a wallpapered side of the room and poured a glass of water from a pitcher. She crossed back to Ford and gave him the half-filled glass which he nearly dropped.

'Here, let me help.'

She leaned against him, putting her arm about his shoulders while the other hand held the glass to his lips. He couldn't help but feel the suppleness of her body.

Once he'd had enough, he asked her name.

'Mary,' she replied.

'Where am I?' Ford asked.

'The Joy Club,' Mary told him.

Ford frowned. 'How? Why? How long? What happened?'

It all tumbled out in a jumble of words.

'Whoa, handsome,' Mary said. 'One at a time. First off, you got yourself shot.'

Ford's mind started to process the information and things began to come back to him. The gunfight in the saloon. The bounty Harper put on his head, and the shot that smashed into his chest. The shot fired by Camilla.

He rubbed absently at his chest and found bandages wrapped firmly around his torso.

'Why am I here?' Ford asked Mary.

'Camilla had them bring you here,' Mary explained. 'She had me go for the doctor to treat your wound.'

Now he was confused. Why would Cam bring him here after shooting him? It made no sense.

'How long have I been here,' he inquired.

'Three days.'

'In this room?'

'Yep.'

'Your room?'

'Sure is.'

'Where did you sleep?'

'Right there beside you,' Mary informed him. 'It's big enough for two.'

'Why?' Ford asked.

Mary frowned. 'Why what?'

'Why did Cam bring me here after she shot me?'

'I guess you'll have to ask her that yourself,' Mary said.

'I guess I will.'

'I'll fetch her for you,' Mary said and disappeared from the room.

It was a small room, or maybe the size of the bed made it seem that way. Its furnishings were few but uncommon to your run of the mill whorehouse, more expensive instead of cheap rubbish.

The door opened again and Camilla walked into the room.

'Mary tells me you want to see me.'

'What the hell am I doin' here?' Ford grated.

'A "thank you" would go down a lot better,' Camilla said.

'You damned well shot me, again,' Ford pointed out.

'What I did was save your life,' Camilla shot back. 'If Ike had shot you, you'd be dead and buried about now. Actually, you are.'

Ford frowned.

'Ike thinks you're dead and that you've been buried in

97

the cemetery,' Camilla explained. 'If he finds out you're still alive and that I was the one who kept you that way, he'll kill us both.'

'So, why do it? I don't understand.'

'Because seeing you again brought back old emotions,' Camilla told him. 'I don't know why. I told myself I hated you for what you did to my brother. But here we are and the feelings are real.'

Ford could understand what she was saying. Seeing Camilla had stirred his feelings as well. Then an alarming thought entered his mind and he struggled to sit up.

'Eddie,' he gasped.

Camilla put a restraining hand upon his chest. 'She's fine. I am hiding her too. I can get her if you want.'

Ford lay back, relieved. 'Maybe later. At least she's safe.'

'You both are, for the moment.'

'What has Cordis been up to while I've been out to it?' Ford inquired.

'It's been business as usual,' Camilla said. 'The mine's reopened. The ranchers tried to stop it and there was a fight. Some of the hands were killed before the miners drove them off.'

'Is Krouse OK?' Ford asked.

'Yes, why?'

'No reason, I liked him is all,' he told her.

Camilla's face grew stern. 'You're up to something, Josh Ford. I know that look you get. There's something going on in that head of yours.'

He'd seen the look many times before and for a moment, he forgot why he was in Serenity in the first place and what Camilla was doing here.

'Cam,' he said in a soft voice, 'I. . . .'

Her eyes softened. 'What?'

He wanted to take her in his arms and kiss her. Pretend that it all had never happened. Then the moment was gone.

'I'm goin' to kill that son of a bitch when I get outta here,' he snarled. 'You see if I don't.'

With a cry of despair, Camilla threw up her hands and stormed from the room. Ford watched her go. He could call her back, he thought, say sorry.

'Cam!' he called after her and waited a moment.

Her figure filled the doorway. 'What?'

'I'm sorry.'

Camilla hurried towards him, the look on her face made him think that she may shoot him again. When she reached him, she kissed him. Hard, passionately, with all of her pent up feelings. When they parted, she stared into his eyes, then turned away and left the room.

Now Ford had one more thing to add to his long list of problems.

CHAPTER 11

'Have you found out who it was yet, or not?' Cordis asked Sam Beck three days after the incident in the saloon. 'Surely by now, you must have some idea?'

Beck nodded. 'It was Kile.'

'The storekeeper?'

Beck nodded.

'Then I suggest we go and pay him a visit,' Cordis said, coming erect from his seat. 'After all, it was him who started the mess that we now find ourselves in. And search amongst the miners and rail workers for men who can use a gun. I've a feeling that we'll be visited by the marshals soon and I don't want to be caught out. Around ten should do.'

'I'll take care of it.'

'Good. Now, let's go and see that damned storekeeper.'

When Kile saw them approaching him in the empty store, he knew instantly that he was a dead man. He ducked below the counter and brought up a .45 caliber Schofield he had sequestered there.

He fumbled nervously with it but by the time he had it

under control, Beck had drawn and fired his Colt. The slug smashed into Kile's arm, the impact causing his hand to open and the six-gun dropped to the floor with a dull thud.

A cry of pain escaped the storekeeper's lips and a desperate look of fear overtook his face.

Cordis shook his head in a display of mock disappointment. 'Clarence, Clarence, what am I going to do with you?'

'Please don't kill me,' he pleaded.

'Oh, I'm afraid we're past that,' Cordis told him. 'The question is, how am I going to do it?'

'Please, no!'

'Don't worry, Clarence,' Cordis said, a wicked smile on his face. 'You won't feel a thing, eventually.'

Kile's body was found later that afternoon. He had been drowned in a barrel of molasses.

'How are you feelin' today, Marshal?' Mary asked sincerely. 'I hope I didn't keep you awake too much last night?'

'No, I don't think someone as soft as you to snuggle into would ever keep me awake,' Ford said, giving her a cheeky grin.

Mary rested a long-fingered hand on his arm. He sat in a chair and had cracked the curtain slightly so that he could look out the dust-smeared window.

'If you ever want more than comfort,' she said seductively, 'I could let you have it for free.'

Ford smiled broadly at the invitation. 'What would your boss say to that?'

'I wouldn't tell her,' answered Mary.

'I'm sure you wouldn't,' Ford allowed. 'What are they

all up to this mornin'?'

Mary suddenly went silent.

'What is it?'

The door opened and Eddie filled the doorway. 'Have you heard?'

'Heard what?' Ford asked impatiently, his confused gaze flicking from Eddie to Mary and back. 'What is it?'

'Clarence Kile was killed yesterday afternoon,' Eddie told him as she closed the door behind herself.

'Who did it?'

Eddie shrugged. 'No one knows. But we can guess.'

'Cordis,' sighed Ford in frustration.

'I take it nobody heard any shooting?' Ford asked.

Mary blanched at the thought of Kile's death.

'Nobody heard any shot because they didn't shoot him,' Eddie told him. 'The bastards drowned him in a barrel of molasses.'

'Damn them,' Ford cursed and began to get to his feet.

'What are you doing?' Eddie asked.

'I'm goin' back to work,' he stated.

'You can't, you aren't ready,' Eddie pointed out.

Ignoring their protests, Ford stood up and the room started to spin. He grabbed the back of the chair to steady himself and sat back down.

'Damn it,' he cursed out loud.

'You still need a few more days,' Eddie cautioned him.

Ford sat and thought for a moment. He didn't like it but knew he was going to need help. And that help was around five days away.

'I need someone to send a wire to Lander for me,' said Ford.

'Why Lander?' Eddie asked.

102

Ford told her.

'That's still days away,' she said.

'I know that,' Ford told her. 'But they're the closest help to us right now. If Cordis unites the miners and the rail workers, then this town will be beyond help.'

'I'll do it.'

The three of them looked at the doorway and saw Camilla standing there. They'd not even heard the door open.

'What about Cordis?' Ford asked her.

'What about him?'

'Why would you want to do it anyway?' Ford asked.

Camilla looked hurt at the question. 'If you don't know why now, then you never will. Let me know when you want it sent.'

Ford seethed inside as he watched her leave. Partly because of the death of Kile. Mostly because of the feelings the damned woman stirred up within him.

'Hell and damnation,' he muttered.

'Why aren't I surprised,' Bass Reeves muttered bitterly and tossed the creased piece of paper on the polished table-top. He looked up at Roy Willis. 'Well, I guess we'd better go and pull his chestnuts out of the fire before he goes and gets himself shot up even more.'

'It must be bad if he's askin' for help,' Willis observed.

'Get the boys ready and we'll be gone within the hour,' Reeves ordered. 'There's still a good few hours before dark.'

Willis hurried away to gather the few marshals who remained in town. There were three of them. The other two had been released to tend other duties once Mason

Fox had been locked away.

'That boy will be the death of me yet,' Reeves muttered.

'What's that, sugar?' a saloon harlot asked him as she walked past his table.

Reeves looked up at her. Her face was layered with makeup and there were large red circles of paint on her cheeks.

Reeves climbed to his feet. 'I said, don't have any kids.'

He left her there trying to figure out his cryptic advice, and walked from the saloon, a dark cloud of worry on his face.

'Somethin's not right, Bass,' Roy Willis commented as he dropped his hand to the butt of his six-gun.

'Ain't that the truth,' Reeves growled and mirrored Willis' action.

The infuriating part about the situation was that they'd not even left Lander yet.

'I got a suspicious lookin' character up on my left, Bass,' a young marshal who rode directly behind Reeves said in a low voice.

The senior marshal looked and saw the man. 'I got him.'

'I got another on my right, Bass,' Willis commented.

'Yeah, got him too.'

'What do you reckon they're up to?' Willis asked.

'Could be anythin',' Reeves allowed. 'All of them no good.'

It wasn't until they'd ridden a few more yards that they found out. As they drew level with the sheriff's office, a large explosion from within seemed to rock the whole town.

The window and parts of the front wall blew out, spraying the street and boardwalk with glass and wicked splinters. A passing pedestrian was blown off the boardwalk and on to a hitch rail and lay motionless, draped over it with a razor-sharp sliver of glass jutting from his back.

The marshals' horses reared and bucked violently as they were showered with debris. One of the lawmen fell from his rearing mount, a wooden splinter embedded in his throat, the ghastly wound pumping blood around the jagged protrusion.

Reeves and Willis fought to bring their mounts under control as they reared violently in the middle of the street.

Next came gunfire. A staccato of shots rang out and bullets snapped close to the remaining marshals. Reeves managed to get his six-gun out of its holster and thumbed back the hammer. He searched for a target and saw one of the men pointed out to him before the explosion.

Knowing how low the chances were of hitting anybody from the back of his prancing horse, Reeves lay down some rapid covering fire then slid from the back of his horse. As he suspected, none of the shots hit their intended target but he saw the man flinch to avoid slivers of wood sprayed from an awning upright next to him.

'Bass, the front of the jail!' Willis cried out.

Reeves looked and saw three figures emerge from the smoking rubble. Two of them he'd never seen before. The other was Mason Fox.

'The bastards are breakin' him outta jail, Roy!' Reeves exclaimed. 'Put them down!'

The gunfire increased and more by luck than anything else, one of the outlaws fell. Reeves tried to sight on Fox but when he squeezed the trigger the hammer fell on a spent cartridge.

'Son of a bitch,' he cursed. 'Roy, you gotta get off your damned bronc so you can get a better shot at them.'

'I'm with you, Bass,' Willis agreed.

Willis came out of his saddle and joined Bass behind his, and then they ran together to find cover. Willis took a knee behind a water trough while Reeves found shelter in the mouth of an alley. Bass reloaded while slugs flew all about. A cry from out on the street signalled another marshal down. Yet almost straight away, an outlaw died with lead in his chest from Willis.

Gunsmoke hung heavy in the late afternoon air as the intensity of the shooting increased. Reeves figured that there were at least three outlaws throwing lead at them, maybe more. He pulled back as a slug chewed splinters from the corner of the bank building where he was hugging the wall. He fired three fast shots before he needed to reload.

While he did, he heard Roy curse loud enough to be heard over the shooting, as a bullet slapped him hard in his left leg. The deputy marshal sprawled on to the ground beside the now leaking water trough.

'Are you OK, Roy?' Reeves called out.

'Yeah, my Grandma whupped me worse when she caught me stealin' her fresh baked cookies.'

'Did you see where Fox went?'

'I think he's over near the mercantile,' Willis said.

'Yeah, he's pinned down behind that barrel,' shouted another deputy.

'I need to change position to get a better shot at him,' Reeves called to Willis.

'You go; I'll cover you.'

Reeves broke cover and ran across the alley mouth, climbed the stairs on to the boardwalk and clomped noisily along the timbers until he found a pile of crates to hide behind. He was almost there when he felt a slug tear through the fleshy part of his upper left arm.

Reeves gritted his teeth against the burning pain.

'Son of a bitch,' he cursed. 'That hurts.'

Ignoring the pain, Reeves raised his six-gun and drew a bead on the barrel where Fox was hiding. He fired one shot that sprayed the outlaw with small wooden chips and saw him reel back. He fired again and saw the shirtsleeve jerk and a small spray of blood erupt from the wound.

'Bass, on your left!' one of the other marshals shouted.

Reeves turned and saw the outlaw coming at him. He swivelled his hips and brought up his gun to fire. He squeezed the trigger and the outlaw stopped as though he'd run into an invisible wall. Then the wall disappeared and he fell on his face, unmoving at Reeves' feet.

Another slug burned across Reeves' ribs with enough force to spin him half around.

'Damn it. Enough of this horse crap,' he fumed as pain spread its long fingers throughout his body.

He broke cover and picked up the fallen outlaw's six-gun. 'Get the hell up, Roy. Let's kill these sonsofbitches.'

Willis struggled to his feet, pain lancing through his wounded leg. They began a methodical gunfire where they moved and selected their targets. Outlaws started to fall under the withering fire. Off to his right, Reeves saw one of his men join in their deadly fight. Near the water barrel, Fox leaped up and started to run. Reeves sighted down his own six-gun barrel and let loose a shot. Through the blue-grey smoke that spewed forth, the marshal saw the scared killer throw up his hands and dive forward.

'Got you, you son of a bitch,' Reeves snarled and turned to look for another target. But there were no more. The gunfight, which had begun as a jailbreak, was over.

The results weren't known immediately, but the figures mounted to eight outlaws dead, Fox amongst them, and one wounded. Four townsfolk were killed, including the town sheriff, and two others were wounded. Reeves, Willis and one other marshal named Clay Meredith were the only ones to live through the furious onslaught, and all of them were wounded in one way or another.

Reeves cursed and started to walk along the street, blood soaking his shirt while some of the bright-red fluid dripped from the fingers of his left hand.

'Where are you goin', Bass,' Willis called after him.

'The telegraph office,' Reeves grouched without turning around. 'I gotta let Josh know he's on his own.'

CHAPTER 12

Ford read the message, screwed the piece of paper up into a tight ball, then threw it at the wall.

'Bad news?' Eddie asked.

'Bass and the others were involved in a shootout in Lander,' Ford explained, disgust tinging his voice. 'They ain't comin'. We're on our own.'

'What now? Are we going to leave town?'

Ford stared out the window and down at the street near the livery. He thought long and hard.

'No. After dark, I'm goin' back to work. The first thing I aim to do is shut down the Dead Dog. If Cordis wants a war, then he'll get one.'

'But you're only one man,' Eddie pointed out. 'Even with my help, we'll still be outgunned.'

Ford's face grew stony. 'You stay out of this. What comes next is nothin' for a woman to be involved in.'

Eddie opened her mouth to protest but Ford shut her down. 'I know what they did to your brother and I'm sorry for that. But I can't take you along on this. It'll be a distraction I can't afford. You'll need to be able to kill a man without compunction, without question and I'm not sure you can.'

He could see the disappointment on her face. 'Stay here out of sight. I'm goin' to be around but not at the jail. From now on I'm not lockin' anyone up. By the time this is over I'll either be dead, or Cordis will be.'

'But you just can't. . . .' Eddie protested.

'Can't what?'

They turned and saw Camilla standing in the doorway.

'Don't you believe in knocking?' Ford asked, dismissively.

'Can't what?' she repeated the question.

'He says he's going back to work,' Eddie explained.

'They'll kill you, Josh,' Camilla said, unable to hide her concern.

'That's what I told him,' Eddie echoed.

'You're the only one who's come close to that,' he pointed out. 'Do you plan on shootin' me a third time?'

'If it will keep you safe, yes.'

'Can I rely on you to get some things for me?'

'What?'

'My guns, ammunition, some other bits 'n' pieces.'

'Make me up a list and I'll get it for you,' Camilla told him. 'What about your horse?'

'I'll fix him myself after dark,' Ford told her.

'But where are you going to stay if not at the jail?' Eddie asked.

'I'll be around,' Ford said. 'Which is more than I can say about Cordis.'

'Oh, Josh,' Camilla said, exasperated. 'How on earth are you going to stop him?'

Ford smiled wryly. 'First I'm goin' to make him good and mad. And then I'm goin' to kill him.'

*

When Ford walked into the Dead Dog saloon sometime after ten that night, the whole barroom looked as though they'd seen a ghost. The man standing before them was dressed in black and aside from the Peacemaker in his holster, his hands also held the messenger gun that they'd become used to him carrying. Tucked into his belt were two more six-guns and hooked over his left shoulder by a leather strap was a Winchester rifle.

The silence was so complete that Ely Cramer came out from his office to see what was happening.

The instant he laid eyes on Ford he gasped and said, 'You're dead. You can't be alive.'

Ford looked around the room. 'It looks like you got yourself some new guns.'

He counted at least three armed men around the room.

'What do you want?' Cramer asked, apprehension in his tone.

'Get everybody out,' Ford ordered.

'What?'

Ford saw one of the new guards move off to his left. With blinding speed, Ford released the messenger gun with his right hand and palmed up his Colt. The weapon roared and the would-be killer staggered with a blossom of red on his shirtfront.

Taking deliberate aim, Ford fired a second shot, which knocked him on to his back. Shouts of alarm filled the room and Ford locked his gaze once more on Cramer.

'Get everybody out, Cramer,' he said in a menacing voice. 'You have exactly one minute.'

111

'Or what?' asked the pale-faced manager.

Ford dropped the Peacemaker into its holster and pulled the stick of dynamite that he'd threatened them all with before he was shot the last time, from his pocket. 'I'm not foolin', Cramer. Get them out.'

'You're a lawman,' the manager said confidently. 'You can't do that.'

Remaining silent, Ford reached into his opposite pocket and retrieved a book of matches. Without any fuss, he took one and lit it. Then he placed it against the dynamite's fuse until it spluttered into life.

'He's goin' to do it!' a miner shouted and started a grand exodus of pushing and shoving bodies.

Ford doused the fuse and waited until the Dead Dog was empty. Almost empty. Cramer still stood in front of him, defiance etched on his face. He nodded towards the extinguished fuse and said, 'I told you; you couldn't do it. You may not be dead yet, but Cordis will kill you and I'll be standin' there to see him do it.'

'Maybe,' Ford allowed, 'but that depends.'

'On what?'

Ford relit the fuse with another match, tossing the deadly blasting implement behind the long hardwood bar. He turned and started to walk towards the street. As he went he said nonchalantly, 'On how fast you can run.'

Cramer charged past Ford who had almost reached the door. His shouts of alarm sent everyone outside scattering for cover. As they watched from their assorted sheltered positions, they witnessed something that could only be described as surreal.

As Ford stepped from the boardwalk down into the street, the dynamite exploded. The glass of the front window blew out, a large orange ball of flame in its wake, escaping from within, while the rest of the building seemed to implode on itself, leaving a pile of burning rubble. The sound resonated across Serenity as though the sky above it had been torn asunder by some invisible giant.

Pieces of timber rained down upon Absaroka Street like man-made hail, and in the middle of it all, a black-clad figure illuminated by a halo of a flaming orange backdrop continued to walk away.

Josh Ford.

When the debris had stopped falling, Cramer raised his head slowly above the rim of a water trough he'd been cowering behind. His jaw dropped when he saw the burning wreck that had once been the Dead Dog saloon. The buildings either side of it were also ablaze. One was the adjoining pool hall that Cordis also owned. The other was, or used to be, a rare commodity: a dentist office. It had been abandoned because the previous tenant had been shot by a disgruntled customer.

Cramer looked about for the man who'd caused the chaos but Ford was nowhere to be seen. The saloon manager swallowed hard. What was Ike Cordis going to say?

Two gunshots close together slapped against the walls of the back room in the Royal Palace saloon and those present heard their ears ring. Cramer jerked violently as the sound echoed in his head. He watched the two remaining guards from the Dead Dog drop to the timber floor, shot through the heart, and the ringing continued.

The six-gun in Ike Cordis' fist moved to its left and centered on Cramer's chest.

'No, wait!' he blurted out, arm outstretched, palm facing the irate man who was about to kill him, as though it could stop the bullet that was about to end his life.

'Why?' Cordis snarled.

'There was nothin' could be done to stop it, Ike, honest,' Cramer pleaded. 'He was supposed to be dead. How is it that he's still alive?'

Cordis thought for a moment and as he did so, the anger surging through him abated. He leathered the six-gun and said, 'You're right. For Ford to have survived that gunshot, he would've needed a doctor. Sam, have a couple of men find him and bring him here.'

Beck nodded.

'One more thing. Put it around that I'm goin' to pay $2,000 for that sonofabitch's head. Let's see how long he stays alive with that hangin' over him.'

The explosion jarred Judge Lemuel Jackson from his slumber but he thought nothing of it. Serenity nights were full of noises: gunshots, shouts, and all kinds of other things. For some reason, though, he had trouble returning to sleep. He tossed and turned for about half an hour when he became aware of a presence in his room. He rolled over and reached for his bedside cupboard only to feel the cold, hard barrel of a gun press against the side of his head.

'You got five minutes to get some clothes on and get the hell outta town,' a voice hissed.

'Don't shoot me,' Jackson bleated. 'I'm a judge.'

'You're no more a judge than I am,' the voice hissed. 'Now move.'

The overweight man rolled out of bed and found his clothes, all the while careful not to look at the face of the man in his bedroom. When he was dressed, Ford lit the lamp beside the bed. The orange light illuminated his face and Jackson's eyes immediately grew wide.

'You,' he gasped. 'You're dead.'

'Not hardly,' Ford said. Then he had a thought. 'Where does Cordis keep all of his money?'

'I – I don't know,' Jackson lied.

The gun hammer ratcheted back, bringing an alarmed expression to Jackson's fleshy face.

'Wait, he keeps it at Ike's Place,' he said hurriedly. 'That's where most of the gambling happens. There's a safe in Bale's office.'

'Does it have a back door?'

'Yes.'

'Good,' Ford nodded. 'Now get out of town. If I ever see you again, I'll see that you end up in a federal pen.'

At the livery twenty minutes later, Jackson had managed to saddle a horse in preparation for his departure from Serenity. It wasn't his horse; he didn't own one. But any horse would do to get him as far away as possible from this town.

He led the sturdy-looking bay outside and managed to drag his large frame into the saddle. He sat atop it and kicked it in the ribs with his heels.

'Come on, horse,' he urged it but the animal remained immobile.

'Damnit, horse, move!'

Nothing.

'God damn ornery son of a bitch—'

'Goin' somewhere, Judge?' a voice asked from the shadows.

Jackson jumped and almost fell from the saddle, his head whipped around. 'Who, me? Nothing. Nothing at all.'

'A little late to be goin' ridin' ain't it?' the man asked. 'Come to think of it, I ain't never seen you on a horse before.'

'I – I, ahh . . .' Jackson stammered.

The triple-click of a gun hammer going back made Jackson kick furiously at the horse, which still refused to budge.

'Get off the horse, Judge,' the man's voice came in a harsher tone this time. 'I think we better go and see Cordis. I think he'll be mighty interested to hear why it is you're tryin' to leave town.'

CHAPTER 13

Ike Cordis listened intently to what Jackson was telling him. The jabbering idiot was hard to understand so he concentrated his gaze on the man's face, willing him to finish. The judge, however, kept glancing at the bloody figure of the town doctor and pausing his story, forgetting where he was up to. The medic was tied to the chair beside him and a large man worked him over with fists covered in blood.

The more he stopped and started, the darker Cordis' mood became. When the judge mentioned that he had told Ford where the money was kept, Cordis shot him where he stood. Four times.

'What the hell is happening to this town?' Cordis raged. 'Come on, Sam, we got to get to that money before Ford does.'

Before he rushed out the door, he looked down at the unmoving form of the corpulent man and shot him again.

When Mort Bale entered his office, the last thing he expected to see was Josh Ford sitting in his leather-backed chair, feet resting on the polished timber desk. He opened his mouth to shout but the sight of Ford's Peacemaker made the shout die in the back of his throat.

'Just come in and lock the door behind you,' Ford ordered. 'We wouldn't want any interruptions now, would we?'

Bale did as he was told and turned back to face Ford. 'What now?'

'Put the key on the desk.'

Bale tossed it and it landed on the hardwood top with a metallic clunk.

Ford indicated to the Mosler safe in the far corner. 'Unlock it.'

'What? Why?'

'Because I want what's in it,' Ford snapped, coming to his feet. 'What the hell do you think I want?'

'No,' Bale said confidently. 'And you won't shoot me because you need me to open it.'

'You know what? You're right,' Ford agreed and shot him in the foot. 'Open the damned safe.'

Bale screamed. The slug had punched through his shoe and foot and embedded itself in the wooden floor.

Ford hurried forward and grabbed him by the collar. 'Open the damned safe or I'll shoot you in the knee next time.'

Moaning with pain, Bale started to spin the small wheel on the front of the safe. First one way then the other until he could pull the heavy door open.

'There you go, you son of a bitch,' Bale said through teeth clenched against the pain that radiated from his foot up his leg. 'When Ike gets hold of you, he'll kill you slow for takin' his money.'

Ford removed an empty burlap sack from inside his

118

coat and started to fill it with everything he could carry. All the notes went in, along with some of the gold. He couldn't take it all, but what he had would do nicely. He figured there to be around $30,000 worth of mixed currency in the sack.

He stood up then directed his gaze at Bale. 'That should get his attention, don't you think?'

Suddenly the door rattled and a heavy fist pounded on the timber. Muffled voices sounded from the other side and Ford began to move towards the back door.

'I guess it's time I was leavin', Ford observed. 'You tell Cordis I'm sorry I missed him and I hope to catch up with him real soon.'

'You're a dead man Ford, you bastard,' Bale cursed him.

As he was leaving, Ford gave him a wave and said, 'I'd say that once Cordis finds out what happened here, you'll be the dead man long before me. Have a nice life, or what's left of it.'

No sooner had the back door closed than the main office door burst open and Ike Cordis strode through the opening, six-gun in his fist. Sam Beck followed him.

'He's just gone out the back door,' Bale said with urgency. 'If you hurry, you'll get him.'

Beck rushed across to the door, wrenched it open and disappeared out into the darkness. Cordis tore his gaze away from the open safe and fixed it on the wounded manager.

'What happened?'

Bale flinched at the harsh edge to his voice.

'He – he was in here waitin' for me. He must've come through the back door.'

119

'Wasn't it locked?' Cordis asked, demanding an answer.

'I – I don't know. Normally it would be but. . . .'

'But it wasn't and now the son of a bitch has virtually cleaned me out,' Cordis snarled.

Beck returned through the door and looked at his boss. He shook his head. 'He's gone.'

Trembling with rage, the six-gun in Ike Cordis' fist lined up on the center of Bale's forehead.

'No! Wait!'

Bale would never know how close he came to dying at that moment, because the man who'd been working over the doctor chose that moment to enter the room. Cordis gave him a questioning look.

'The doctor talked,' he said in a low voice.

'Who?'

'Camilla.'

'He's lying,' Cordis snorted. 'Go and question him again.'

'I can't. He's dead.'

'Damn it.'

'He wasn't lyin',' the man said. 'He told me so I would stop beatin' on him.'

'It's not true,' Cordis assured him. 'It can't be.'

'She ain't been around much, Ike,' Beck pointed out.

'She's as much a part of this as we all are. I don't believe it,' he stated. 'And I'll prove it. Come on, we're goin' to see her.'

Eddie was torn from her slumber by the sound of raised voices and something breaking. She sat on the side of her lumpy mattress and listened, unsure whether it had come from within the building or out on the street. The room was bathed in silvery moonlight that filtered through the window. She slipped from the bed and stepped lightly across to the door, opened it a crack and listened.

'After all I've done for you, this is the way you repay me?' she heard a man snarl.

'Keep away from me, Ike,' came Camilla's voice, 'or I'll stick you with this knife.'

She heard a maniacal laugh then Camilla screech, 'Keep away from me!'

Eddie shut the door and hurried to where her clothes hung over a chair. She dressed in quick time and strapped her six-gun around her waist. She made sure the gun was fully loaded, cocked the hammer then exited the room into the hallway.

A dull orange glow from a single lamp barely illumi-nated the wooden walls and long carpet runner. The sounds grew louder as Eddie neared the top of the stairs. One of the girls poked her head out of her room and gave her a frightened glance.

Eddie shooed her back in and turned as another girl hurried towards her. The terrified look on her face said it all.

'What's happening?' Eddie whispered.

'It's Ike and Sam Beck,' she blurted out, fear dripping from her voice. 'Ike's gone crazy. He knows Camilla helped the marshal after she shot him. He's going to kill her.'

'Get to your room and lock the door,' Eddie told her. 'Stay there and don't come out.'

The semi-naked girl hurried along to the third door on the right and went inside.

Eddie started to move cautiously down the stairs. Below

her, the sounds continued. The shouts, a woman's cries of alarm, and at one point Eddie heard a meaty thwack resonate up the stairs. A surge of anger ripped through her, and she threw caution to the wind and took the last steps in a couple of strides.

At the bottom of the stairs, Eddie stopped near a door that was ajar and paused. Inside the room, she heard Cordis ask, 'Where is he?'

'I don't know!'

Thwack!

She'd heard enough. Eddie pushed the door open and stepped into the void. Cordis with an upraised hand was ready to strike Camilla another blow. Sam Beck was on the other side of the beaten and bloodied woman, who cowered lower on her wooden chair.

'If you hit her again, you son of a bitch, I'll put a slug in your guts,' Eddie snarled.

Cordis turned to look at Eddie and Beck reached for his gun.

'Don't even think about it, Beck, or you'll get it first,' she hissed at Cordis' right-hand man.

'Get out of here, girl, before you get yourself hurt,' the boss' icy voice sent a shiver down Eddie's spine.

Not letting it show she said, 'No. You let her go, now.'

As if to emphasize her point she lined the six-gun up on his face. 'Camilla, can you walk?'

Camilla nodded as she rose to her feet. 'I'll manage.'

'I'll kill you both,' Cordis hissed.

'Get out the door, Camilla,' Eddie said. 'I'll be right behind you.'

After she had passed her, Eddie slipped the key from inside the door and closed it. She then locked it from the outside. Turning around, she saw Camilla waiting for her inside the main door.

'We have to get out of town,' Eddie told her.

'And go where?'

The heavy crash of boot on wood echoed loudly as their prisoners tried to break free of their prison. Eddie grabbed Camilla by the arm. 'Come on, I have an idea. We'll head to the Rocking K.'

'I can't go there,' Camilla said, coming to a sudden stop. 'They know who I am.'

Another crash and the lock splintered, allowing the trapped men to escape.

Eddie pulled at Camilla's arm. 'Come on, we'll argue about it later.'

Gunshots filled the entryway and slugs chewed wood-chips from the jam and scythed through the empty space not long vacated. The two women moved quickly towards the livery. More gunshots rang out and Camilla grunted under the impact of a leaden slug that bit deep into her back. She staggered and went down.

'Camilla!' Eddie cried out and brought up her six-gun. She fired at the approaching figures making them take cover.

She bent down to check Camilla but found no sign of life. Her mind reeled at the realization that she was dead. There was no time to think about it, as another shot sounded and the bullet fizzed dangerously close overhead. Eddie fired two more shots and began to run in a low crouch, towards the livery where she hoped to find a horse she could steal.

Eddie, however, didn't make it. She tripped over a pro-truding rock and her momentum propelled her forward forcefully, smacking her head into something hard and stunning her.

She lay there momentarily, bright lights before her eyes. She tried to rise, and managed to regain her feet, then toppled forward again, her head a haze of cobwebs. A voice inside her mind screamed at her to get up, but she was incapable of heeding the advice.

She felt rough hands begin to drag her to her feet and a distant voice said, 'Don't kill her. We can use her to get to Ford.'

It was the last thing Eddie Yukon heard at the time because everything went black.

CHAPTER 14

When Father Michael O'Sullivan entered Serenity church the following morning, he was not expecting to see a man pointing a gun at him. Especially a man with a badge pinned to his chest.

'I see that the Lord has seen fit to guide a dead man to his house,' O'Sullivan said, then nodded at the Peacemaker. 'You'll not be needing that in here.'

Ford dropped it into his holster and apologized. 'Sorry Father, you can't be too careful around here.'

O'Sullivan nodded his understanding. 'It be a pit infested with snakes for sure. But one day maybe, God will send us a prophet to rid us of the evil that ravages our fair town.'

'Will I do?' Ford jested.

O'Sullivan sighed. 'It seems you may have to. Have you ever heard of the phoenix, Marshal Ford?'

'Only vaguely,' Ford admitted.

'It is said that the phoenix is a beautiful bird that rises from the ashes of what it once was,' O'Sullivan explained. 'I fear that may be true for our Serenity also.'

Ford frowned. 'You mean burn the town?'

'Not literally, Marshal Ford, metaphorically,' O'Sullivan said. 'First, the bad element must be removed before the new town can grow and blossom into something even better than it once was.'

'That's what I'm tryin' to do,' Ford told him.

'It seems that whatever you are doing is working. The snakes are turning on themselves. Why, last night they killed one of their own.'

'Who?'

'The woman.'

Ford felt as though he had been punched in the gut and all the air forced from his lungs. His mind reeled and he thought for a moment that he'd misheard what O'Sullivan had said.

'What do you mean?'

'Apparently, they had a falling out last night over at that den of iniquity the woman ran,' O'Sullivan explained. 'There were two women involved. The woman they call Camilla was shot and killed by one of the men. The woman who was your deputy was taken by them to the Royal Palace. It appears that they didn't take too kindly to you blowing up the Dead Dog, which has set in motion a violent chain of events. Ike Cordis not only killed the two guards from that saloon but he also killed our *esteemed* judge.'

'Are you sure he shot Camilla?'

'Yes.'

'God damn it to hell,' Ford cursed, then remembered where he was. He shot a glance at O'Sullivan and said, 'Sorry, Father.'

'I couldn't have said it better myself.'

Ford's thoughts switched to Eddie. There'd be time

enough later to reflect on Camilla's fate. At this moment, Eddie needed him more than a dead madam did.

'Can you do somethin' for me, Father?' Ford asked.

'I'll try.'

'I need you to take a message to Cordis for me. Can you do that?'

He nodded. 'I can do that. He hasn't taken to killing men of the cloth just yet.'

'You might want to hear the rest of it before you agree.'

Bass Reeves walked into the Lander livery and stopped dead in his tracks.

'About time you got here,' Roy Willis said, as he limped around his horse to finish adjusting his saddle. 'We were thinkin' we might have to leave without you.'

Reeves looked across the horse's rump at Clay Meredith, who was doing the same as Willis.

'Where the hell do you all think you're goin'?' Reeves grumbled. The pain from his wounds made him more irritable than usual.

'The same place as you,' Willis told him. 'To help Ford.'

'We're goin' to have to ride like the dickens if we're to get there in time,' Reeves pointed out. 'Can your leg stand it?'

'It'll stand it for as long as I can,' Willis assured him.

'What about you?' he asked the other man.

'I'll be fine, Bass. It only hurts when I move.'

The tough marshal felt a surge of pride flow through him. Here were two men, both wounded, yet still willing to go the extra mile to help him, and a fellow marshal, out of trouble. Then he dismissed it as being the emotions of a fool.

'Where's my damned horse?' he grouched. 'It's time we were gone.'

Twenty minutes later the three marshals, wounds and all, rode hell-for-leather out of Lander, hoping that they would not be too late.

'He what?' Cordis asked disbelief etched on his face.

'He says he has your money and is willing to trade it for the woman,' O'Sullivan repeated. 'But it will be tomorrow at the church at 9 o'clock.'

Cordis thought about it a moment and then the penny dropped. Tomorrow was Sunday and the church would be packed with parishioners. 'You tell him it ain't going to happen that way.'

'He said you'd probably say that,' O'Sullivan told him. 'He said to give you this.'

O'Sullivan held out a small sack for Cordis to take. The killer did so and opened it up. At first, he wasn't sure what he was looking at, but then he figured from the burnt smell that it was ashes. Frowning, he reached in and pulled out a handful. It was crunchy but powdery. Something caught in his fingers, a larger piece of what he assumed to be paper.

Which is what it was. The paper was printed on. Cordis looked at it briefly before he looked back at the priest.

'The marshal said he would do the same to the rest of it if you couldn't meet his terms.' O'Sullivan explained further.

Cordis' eyes grew cold. 'You tell him that if he doesn't meet my terms, then I shall kill the woman.'

'The marshal figures that there is somewhere in the vicinity of $29,000 left. He also figures that you'll be wanting it back more than you'll be wanting to kill the woman.'

'He's bluffin',' Beck growled.

'I guess we'll find out,' Cordis said. 'All right, preacher, tell him we'll be there.'

After O'Sullivan had left the saloon, Beck said, 'Surely you can't be serious, Ike?'

Cordis shoved the small sack into Beck's hands. 'The son of a bitch has most of my money. If he don't get the woman back, this is what'll happen to the rest of it. Take a look.'

Beck looked in the sack then back at his boss. 'He won't burn the rest of it, Ike. He knows we'll kill the woman if he does.'

'Well, I ain't goin' to take that risk,' Cordis told him. 'Tomorrow while we're inside trading for the money, I want men all around that damn church so they can't get away.'

'I can't see why we just can't go get the son of a bitch now and be done with it,' Beck said. 'He's gotta be at the church.'

'Leave it until tomorrow, Sam. That way everyone present will see what happens when people interfere.'

'What did he say?' Ford asked O'Sullivan as he came through the large timber double-doors, the thud as they closed resonating across the empty pews.

'He said he would do it,' the preacher informed him. 'You do realize that once he gets his money, he'll do everything he can to kill you? How do you plan to get out of here once you have the woman back? He'll surround this place with men to stop you.'

Ford nodded. 'If you have an idea on that, I'd like to hear it.'

'Maybe I have,' O'Sullivan told him. 'It may not work, though. It's not quite a plan. However, it's better than the one you have now.'

O'Sullivan went on to tell Ford about his thoughts on the subject. When he'd finished, Ford said, 'I hope it works. If it don't. . . .'

'If it doesn't work then I guess the Lord will take care of you.'

Ford gave him a wry smile. 'Trust me, Father, I'm sure he'd take one look at me and send me on my way.'

'I'm sure he realizes that it takes all kinds of good people to make the world go around.'

'Let's hope so,' Ford said. 'I would ask one more thing of you, though.'

'What's that?'

'Get everyone that you can, safely out of town,' Ford told him.

O'Sullivan frowned. 'Why?'

'There's a storm comin' Father, and I don't want any innocent people gettin' hurt.

'I'm sure they'll survive it, Marshal,' O'Sullivan told him. 'They've weathered storms before.'

'Not like this one, Father. Not like this one.'

When Cordis and Beck entered the confines of the small room, Eddie was laying on the floor struggling with her bonds. The dark curtains were drawn which made the room above the main barroom of the Royal Palace very dim.

'Struggle all you like, you won't get free.'

'Let me go, you murdering bastard,' Eddie hissed. 'If I get loose from here, I'll damn well kill you.'

'Calm down, Missy. . . .'

'Don't you damn "missy" me,' she growled.

'If you let me finish . . . You should be outta here come 9 o'clock tomorrow. It seems that the marshal values you more than my money.'

Eddie stopped struggling, unsure whether Cordis was telling the truth.

'You mean to tell me that once he hands over the money, you're letting us go?' she asked sceptically.

'Oh no,' he said, giving her a knowing smile. 'I said nothing about letting you both go. I just said that you'd be out of here. I still aim to kill you both.'

'Son of a bitch.'

'Got it in one.'

CHAPTER 15

When the assigned time came the following morning, the church was packed, an air of tension encompassed all within. However, when the door crashed back and Ike Cordis entered, everyone knew that something bad was about to happen.

'Where is the son of a bitch who has my money?' he called at the top of his voice.

Behind him, Eddie gave a cry of alarm as she stumbled through the opening after a shove by Sam Beck.

O'Sullivan stood behind his pulpit, staring blankly at Cordis and his hired killer.

'Well, I'm waiting damn it,' he snarled.

Ford stood up from the front pew and turned to face him. He also cleared the flap of his coat away from the butt of the Peacemaker.

'I never thought I'd see the day when The Devil would be in the house of the Lord,' Ford scoffed.

'Where's my money?' Cordis demanded, ignoring the barb.

'Send me the girl,' Ford said to him.

'Money first.'

Ford shook his head. 'Not goin' to happen.'

'Don't you trust me?' Cordis sneered.

'Let's just say I trust me more.'

'Let her go, Sam.'

Eddie started forward.

'Just so you know, this place is surrounded by guns. There ain't no way you're getting out of here.'

'Do you think they're willin' to die for you?' Ford asked him.

Cordis remained silent.

Nervous eyes watched as Eddie made her way toward the front of the church. When she reached Ford, the marshal reached down behind the pulpit and tossed the bag of money into the center aisle. Then, without hesitating, Ford drew his Colt and fired two shots into the ceiling of the church.

The reaction of the congregation was instantaneous. They all leapt to their feet and charged towards the exit. In the melee, Ford grabbed Eddie by the hand and dragged her to the back room of the church.

She almost fell down it before she saw the opening in the floor. A trapdoor lid lay open, revealing a gaping dark hole in the timber floorboards.

'Get down there,' Ford snapped.

'What?'

'Get down the hole,' he said again. 'Father O'Sullivan will close us in.'

'You have to be kidding,' Eddie blurted out. 'We'll be like rats in a trap down there.'

'If we walk out the back door, the men Cordis has out

there will shoot us down before we get ten yards,' Ford grated, taking her by the arm. 'Now get your ass down there before they come.'

'If you get me killed I'll never talk to you again,' Eddie warned him.

'You'll be fine,' he told her as he followed her down the steps.

'What makes you so sure?'

O'Sullivan closed the trapdoor and the darkness became total.

'Because if you get killed,' Ford whispered, 'it'll mean that I got killed too. And I ain't got time to die. Not today.'

There was a loud dragging sound overhead as O'Sullivan put the table back where it had been. No sooner had he done so than a commotion signalled the arrival of Cordis and Beck.

'Where the hell are they?' he snarled in a loud voice.

'I do not know. When I came in, there was nobody here,' he waved his right arm around for emphasis.

Cordis shouldered past him. 'Get the hell outta my way.'

For the next hour, sounds of the search filtered down through the floor into the dark void where Ford and Eddie were hiding. Eventually, it all went quiet and a few minutes later, the scraping sounded again and the trapdoor swung open to reveal one Father O'Sullivan.

'It seems you are safe for the moment,' he told them.

'Yes, but for how long?' Eddie asked.

Ford climbed from the darkness and said, 'I don't aim to hang around to find out. Father, I'll give you until the day after tomorrow to get the people outta here.'

134

O'Sullivan nodded. 'I'll do my best.'

'What happens then?' Eddie inquired.

Ford's voice grew grave. 'Then I'm comin' back, and Hell's goin' to burn.'

Cordis looked up from where he sat toying with a half-empty shot glass when Beck entered the back room of the Royal Palace. The gunfighter had been searching the town for most of the day, with the help of miners and rail workers, trying to find Ford and Eddie.

'I'm not even going to ask,' he snorted.

'It's like they disappeared into thin air,' Beck told him.

'A man can't just vanish,' Cordis snarled. 'He's in this town somewhere.'

'If I had to make a guess, I would say not for much longer,' Beck told him. 'It seems to me that a lot of folks seem keen to leave all of a sudden. I noticed it earlier while we were searching. It was just a few at first, but now it seems like everyone wants out.'

Confused, Ike Cordis climbed to his feet and walked through the bar room and on to the boardwalk. It wasn't a mass exodus, but it was noticeable. Here and there packed wagons lumbered out of town, some trailed pack-horses or mules.

'Where do you think they're goin'?' Beck asked.

Cordis stared blankly at them for a moment, his mind working. He stepped down from the boardwalk and caught a man walking by, on the arm, startling him.

'Where are you going? Cordis asked him.

The man hesitated before he said, 'We're gettin' outta town.'

'Why?'

The question was met with silence.

Cordis gave the man a shake, a flicker of alarm crossing his face. 'Why, damn it?'

'The preacher said for us to leave,' he blurted out, wanting Cordis to leave him alone. 'He said there's goin' to be a fight soon and for us to get out so we don't all get hurt.'

Cordis shoved him away and he stumbled before righting himself and hurrying off.

'What do you want to do, Ike?' Beck asked.

'We'll go and have a chat to that preacher. He knows more than he's lettin' on.'

The interrogation bore little fruit, but when they'd finished questioning O'Sullivan, they knew as much as he did, which wasn't much at all. Ford and the girl had left town and Ford had plans on coming back the day after tomorrow to bring Cordis' reign to an end.

The pair stood on the steps of the church and watched the procession for a while before Beck asked, 'Do you want me to stop them from leavin'?'

'No. Get over to the livery and see if that bastard blue roan Ford rides is still there. Make sure he's gone. After that, round up some fighting men. As many as you can get. When he comes back, we'll have a nice little surprise waiting for our esteemed United States Deputy Marshal.'

When William Krouse saw riders approaching, he was instantly cautious. He called to the two men he'd posted on guard since the battle with the miners. 'Keep an eye on them.'

As the riders drew close enough to be made out clearly, Krouse shook his head. 'Well, I'll be.'

Ford and Eddie eased their mounts to a stop in the ranch yard and watched Krouse step down from his long verandah. As he did, he called back over his shoulder, 'Helen, we have visitors.'

Krouse stopped in front of the horses and looked at Ford.

'Step down, Marshal,' he greeted. 'I didn't expect to see you out here.'

'I needed help, Krouse, and you're the only man I could think of that might do it,' Ford told the rancher as he and Eddie climbed down.

'I been hearin' a lot of stories about you,' the rancher explained. 'One of them had you as dead.'

'Almost was,' Ford allowed.

Krouse signalled to one of his men. 'Take their horses. Put them in the corral.'

As the man went to take the blue roan, Ford said, 'Take care around him. He'll have the hide off you before you know it.'

The hand thought he was joking at first but when he saw the look in Ford's eyes he knew the lawman was serious.

'Sure. Thanks.'

Ford heard the screen door slam shut and looked over at the veranda. He saw Helen Krouse standing there, a look of apprehension on her face. She was a slim woman and her age seemed to be in line with her husband's.

'Sorry to turn up unannounced, Ma'am,' Ford apologized, 'but we had nowhere else to go.'

'You're welcome to join us for supper when the time comes, Marshal,' she assured him. 'We'd not turn away anyone in need.'

'Thank you, Ma'am.'

'Maybe your lady friend would like to come into the house to freshen up while you men talk business?' she suggested.

Eddie stepped forward. 'Thank you, Mrs Krouse. That would be fine.'

Ford watched her go with the rancher's wife as they went inside. He looked around the large ranch yard. Apart from the house with its large verandah, which was set back amongst some large pines, there was also a split-rail corral, an oversized barn, and a long bunkhouse for all the hands.

'Nice place you have here,' Ford observed.

'We're workin' at it,' Krouse said. 'What is it you want?' Straight to the point.

'A while back you came to me for help. I'm here asking the same of you.'

'I asked you for help because that's your job,' Krouse pointed out.

'Yes, it is,' Ford agreed. 'But do you want to get your town back? Even your valley?'

'Of course.'

'I'm only one man, Krouse. I can't do it without help.'

'What did you have in mind?'

Ford told him his idea. After he'd finished, he paused a moment then added, 'To do it we'll need two wagons.'

Krouse looked at him as though he'd gone mad.

'The wagons I can do. The other stuff I don't have. And I'll need to ask the men because it'll be them layin' down their lives.'

'Fair enough,' Ford nodded. 'If they agree, we'll need someone to keep an eye on the town until we're ready.'

'I'll see to that,' Krouse assured him. 'You haven't said how we're goin' to get the other stuff.'

'We're goin' to steal it from the mine.'

CHAPTER 16

A cloud scudded across the quarter moon, darkening the scarred landscape of the mine that loomed up before the riders. There was a slight high-country chill to the air that pricked the exposed skin. Ford was in the lead, followed by Krouse. Ford had insisted that he stay behind but the rancher would have none of it. There had been no qualms from his men either, eager to join the fight against Ike Cordis. In fact, they relished the idea of paying him back.

Ford guessed that it was somewhere after midnight as they approached the mine. He drew the roan to a stop and the others followed suit. Behind them, he could hear the troublesome squeak and rattle of the wagon as it closed the gap between them.

'You all know what you have to do,' Ford whispered. 'Once we get the dynamite, we'll get out of here. Try not to kill anyone unless absolutely necessary. Chances are they're just guardin' the place.'

There were grumbles from a couple of the riders.

'You heard him,' Krouse whispered harshly. 'Shoot only if you have to.'

They dismounted and moved in cautiously, leaving one man with the wagon and horses.

Twenty minutes later, they had accessed the small wooden structure where the mine had its blasting requirements secured. They restrained the rest of the guards and then brought up the horses and wagon, ready for loading.

Ford indicated the four tied men who sat on the ground, their backs to each other. 'Take them away from here. We don't want them going up with the shack when we blow it.'

'What'll your boss say when he finds out what you've been up to?' Krouse asked.

'He'll turn all shades of colors at first,' Ford chuckled, thinking of Bass. 'Then he'll most likely fire me. But it'll all work out in the end.'

'If he does fire you, I reckon the town will be needing a new sheriff.'

'Let's just see if we can get out of this alive first, and then go from there.'

Some minutes later, a wiry cowhand approached them and said, 'The wagon's loaded and the charges are set.'

'All right, let's get the hell outta here.'

A giant fireball lit the night sky after they'd left. Thunder from the explosion rolled along the valley in what seemed like an unending rumble.

'That'll get their attention,' Krouse said.

'It will, that's for sure. All we need to do now is get ready to fight The Devil on his own ground.'

'Someone hit the mine last night,' Sam Beck said, as he entered the Royal Palace saloon. 'They blew the powder shack to hell an' gone.'

Ike Cordis was having a late breakfast of bacon and eggs.

'Who?' Cordis asked as he placed his knife and fork on the table.

'It was Ford and some cow nurses.'

Cordis thought for a moment as he continued to chew the food in his mouth.

'Did they take anything?'

'They didn't say.'

'Who didn't say?'

'The fellers who just came into town.'

'Go and find out why it was done and whether anything was taken,' Cordis ordered him. 'They wouldn't do that just for the hell of it. Find out why.'

Beck nodded.

'How many men did you get that are willing to fight?'

'Around thirty.'

'And they're not afraid of getting their hands dirty?'

'Not a one.'

'Good. Tomorrow we should be rid of that damned marshal once and for all.'

'The men just got back from town,' Krouse told Ford. 'They're getting ready for us. Someone must have told them.'

Ford paused from looping rawhide cord around sticks of dynamite. 'It don't matter much. I figured they would know somethin' was up when people started leavin' town.'

'Cordis has been recruitin' men too. They think he has around thirty men willin' to fight for him. We only have ten. Includin' me and you.'

'Eleven,' Eddie said as she approached.

'Nope, you're sittin' this one out,' Ford said adamantly.

'I haven't come this far just to "sit it out" as you say. I'm goin'.'

'The hell you are. You're stayin' here.'

The look he gave Eddie made her understand that he wouldn't back down. Instead she nodded, turned and walked away.

'Do you think she'll listen?' Krouse asked.

'Not one bit,' Ford acknowledged. 'Although I hope she's sensible enough to see she don't belong where we're goin'. Speakin' of which, maybe you should stay here too.'

Immediately, Ford wished he'd never uttered the words. Krouse's face changed color and he opened his mouth to protest vehemently when Ford quickly raised his hand.

'Hold on before you blow up and bust,' Ford said. 'Think about it. If somethin' happens to you, your wife will be left all alone. Who's goin' to take care of her?'

'This is still my valley, my town. So, if anyone has a right to fight for it, then it's me.'

'All right then,' Ford nodded. 'Just remember this, not all of us are goin' to make it out alive.'

'I'm quite aware of that fact.'

'All right, we'll go in tomorrow afternoon, late in the day. That way if we get tied down, we can use the cover of dark to pull out.'

'Do you think we'll be able to do it?'

'I guess we'll find out.'

The three marshals hit the small town of Crossover that afternoon, their horses bone tired and about dead on their hoofs. There wasn't much to the town: a main street with a couple of side streets.

Roy Willis broke off from the other two and headed for a rickety looking hitch rail on the right side of the main street.

Bass Reeves hauled back on his reins bringing his mount to a halt.

'What do you think you're doin'?' he asked impatiently.

'We need to stop, Bass,' Willis said.

'The hell you say. We need to keep goin'. A man's life is on the line.'

'I know he's your son, Bass, but our horses are almost dead. If we push them any further we'll kill them before we get another five miles. I know it, and you know it. If we stop here overnight, we'll still make Serenity late tomorrow.'

Reeves cursed out loud and slapped his thigh, sending a puff of trail dust exploding from his pants leg.

'Damn it to hell, Roy. He could be dead by the time we get there.'

'And he could be dead already, Bass,' Willis pointed out. 'One thing is for certain, though, we'll be no use to him if we kill our horses.'

A horse-drawn wagon came to a stop behind Reeves and a voice called to him from the town boardwalk.

'Are you just goin' to sit on your horse blocking the street so no one else can use it?' it asked.

Reeves turned in the saddle and gave the man a withering glare.

'What the hell is it to you?' he snarled.

The man, thinly built with black hair, pulled back his jacket flap to show the badge pinned on his vest. 'The name's Dave Bennett.'

Reeves shook his head and eased his tired horse to one side, allowing the wagon to rattle past on the rutted street.

'You fellers look like you've come far in a hurry,' the lawman observed. 'Is there somethin' I need to know about you all?'

'We're marshals,' Roy Willis informed him. 'We're headed on up to Serenity. Got a man up there who is havin' some trouble with the locals.'

The lawman nodded. 'Uh-huh. I been gettin' reports comin' outta there lately. Seems that the lid's about to blow off the town somethin' fierce. I was talkin' to a feller only an hour or so ago who come down from there. He was tellin' me a bit about your marshal. That Ike Cordis is a bad man up there, so they say. Sounds to me like your feller's got hisself a bear by the tail.'

'Where's this feller you were talkin' to?' Reeves inquired.

'Over at the saloon,' the sheriff said, pointing to a sign that said 'Muddy Waterhole'.

'Can you let him know we'd like a word with him?' Reeves asked. 'We just need to put our horses up for the night.'

'Sure, I can do that.'

'Thanks.'

The saloon was filled with a blue-grey smoke haze, the smell of unwashed bodies and stale alcohol. Scantily clad women weaved in and out of tables, touching and talking to the men, plying them for drinks and other, more personal things. The bar was long and scarred, the tables round and small.

In a far corner, a pianist belted out his rendition of an

unrecognizable song because the piano was so far out of tune.

Reeves, Willis, and Meredith found their man sitting alone at a table near the front window of the establishment. His name was Bassett and he used to have a small saddlery in Serenity. He'd left in a hurry when word came from the local preacher to do so.

'Why was the preacher tellin' everybody to leave?' Reeves asked him.

'Because the marshal was plannin' somethin'.'

'What?'

'I don't know,' Bassett said. 'I don't even know how he's alive after he got shot.'

'He got shot?' Reeves snapped.

'Sure did. The woman shot him.'

Reeves had a feeling that he knew the answer his next question before he asked it. 'What woman?'

'The one called Camilla,' Bassett answered. Then he frowned. 'It was strange because even though she shot him, she was the one who got him doctored. And then Cordis killed her. Then the marshal took Cordis' money and Cordis took the other woman captive.'

'Anythin' else?' Reeves asked.

'It was to be expected, though,' Bassett commented.

'What was?'

'Him getting' shot,' he explained. 'Up until then, Marshal Ford had been goin' through them fellers like a good dose of castor oil. He'd already killed two of Cordis' guns, plus other men he had workin' for him. He hired himself a deputy but one of Cordis' men killed him.'

'Is that it?' Reeves asked again.

'Heck, no. The marshal had that feller cornered in one

146

of Cordis' saloons and he was about to tell the marshal everythin' when Cordis shot him.'

'Who? Ford?' Willis asked.

'No, the feller who shot the deputy,' Bassett said, 'keep up. So then the marshal arrested him and put him on trial for murder but the judge threw it out of court.'

'Why?' asked Reeves.

'Because he was Cordis' man. He even said the miners could go back to work.'

'What was with the miners?'

'The marshal shut the mine down.'

'It seems to me that the marshal has been busy since his arrival in Serenity,' Reeves commented while his gaze settled on Roy Willis.

'Sure has,' Bassett agreed. 'Shame it'll be all for nothin', though.'

'Why's that?' asked Willis.

'He ain't got much chance without any help. I'd say by this time tomorrow he'll be dead.'

Reeves chuckled.

'What's so funny about a man gettin' killed?' Bassett asked indignantly.

'Your statement, Mr Bassett,' Reeves explained. 'The sheriff said somethin' earlier about Ford havin' a bear by the tail. It seems to me that it's the other way around.'

CHAPTER 17

'Is everythin' ready?' Krouse asked Ford as the lawman placed the last bundle of dynamite into a crate.

'Yeah, that was the last one. Are your boys ready?'

'They're ready, all right,' Krouse said with confidence.

'Get them gathered around, I want to have a talk with them before we go.'

A few minutes later the cowhands were in a group in front of Ford.

'Listen up,' he addressed them. 'None of you have to do this, so don't feel like you do. I'm sure no man here would think less of any one of you for pullin' out. After all, there is a good chance that most of us, if not all of us, will get killed.'

Ford paused to let his words sink in. Not one man moved.

'OK then. Tell me your names.'

They looked curiously at him.

'Tell me your names. I want to remember the men who've stood up to fight alongside me.'

A thin man stepped forward and said, 'I'm Burke.'

Another followed suit and said, 'Bishop.'

The rest did the same and Ford now knew the names of them all. Smith, Allen, Cooper, Walters, Timms, Bishop and Burke.

'You men in the first wagon, keep layin' down cover fire as we run along Absaroka Street,' Ford told them. 'You men in the second, get them bundles lit and out. Once we do the run back, dismount and fight on foot. Clear the buildings until all the resistance is gone. If you see Cordis or Beck, kill them. Don't hesitate, they'll do the same thing to you.'

'Why are we destroyin' our town?' the cowhand named Allen asked.

'That's just it. It ain't your town, it's Cordis' town. He's the boss. He's killed anyone who has opposed him, including officers of the law.' Ford's gaze fixed on all of them. 'There could well be townsfolk left in Serenity so be aware of that. But more than likely, if you see anyone carryin' a gun, then treat them as the enemy. Any other questions?'

They remained silent.

'All right, one more thing. Everyone raise your right hand.'

He watched as they did as they were told. 'OK. Repeat after me.'

By the time Ford was finished, all of them had been deputized.

'Get them wagons rollin',' Ford ordered them. 'We're goin' to town.'

Minutes after their departure, another rider left the ranch. One with long red hair.

Ike Cordis stood on the boardwalk outside the Royal Palace and looked along an almost deserted Absaroka

Street. The sun was now descending towards the mountains and the expected attack still hadn't come. This was the second day after the incident in the church. It was also the day Ford had given for the town to be cleared.

'Maybe he ain't comin',' Beck said as he stepped out of the saloon and stood beside his boss.

'He'll come,' Cordis said, sounding certain.

'Well, if they do, they're in for a shock. We got men hid out everywhere along the street. The son of a bitch will be dead before he gets anywhere near this place.'

'Do not underestimate our friend the marshal,' Cordis warned Beck. 'We've done so before and it's come back on us.'

A man appeared, running along Absaroka Street at a good clip. He stopped in front of the two men, blowing hard.

'They're—' he swallowed hard. 'They're here.'

'How many is "they"?' Beck asked.

'I ain't sure. They brought two wagons with them, though.'

'What would they want with two wagons?' Beck wondered aloud.

'I guess we'll find out,' Cordis said. 'Let's go and give them a great big welcome.'

Ford stopped the roan about three hundred yards short of town and studied the scene before him. The wagons rattled to a stop and waited for him to give them guidance. Krouse stepped down from the lead wagon and walked up beside the roan.

'What do you think?'

'I think we should go in and say hello,' Ford said. 'Get

150

them moving.'

Ford waited while they got organized and when they were ready, he removed the Winchester from the saddle scabbard and jacked a round into the breech. He turned in the saddle and called to the two drivers. 'Let's go!'

Ford gave the roan a kick and he leaped forward. The gunfire commenced almost the instant they hit the edge of Serenity. The men in the first wagon returned fire as fast as they could. A bullet from a position to Ford's left snapped close to his ear. A man had taken cover behind some well-placed sacks filled with God knows what.

He snapped a shot in the man's direction and noticed a puff of dust rise from one of the sacks that the bullet struck. Then he looked about and saw that other items had been placed sporadically along the boardwalks to create firing positions.

Things were about to get interesting.

Without much hope of hitting anything from horse-back, the idea was to keep the heads of their enemy down so the thrower could do his job.

Behind him, a hollow boom rang out and the first firing position that Ford had ridden past disintegrated, along with the front of the business and the shooter. Debris was flung in all directions. Large, deadly splinters of wood and glass scythed through the air.

Ahead of Ford, more guns opened up and deadly lead hornets filled the air. He rode through the storm, feeling the tug on the sleeve of his shirt at a near miss.

Unseen behind him, the small band took their first casualty. Smith took a bullet to his chest and fell back into the wagon he was riding in. However, undeterred, the others kept up their rate of fire.

As the attackers drew to the end of their first run, the scene of devastation behind them was clearly visible. As Ford reined in, he turned his horse to survey the scene.

The Royal Palace had taken a direct blast, along with Ike's Place and the Pink Garter, as they concentrated their assault on establishments owned by Ike Cordis. Smoke was already starting to rise as flames took hold of the destroyed buildings.

There were some other businesses damaged; the result of dynamite being thrown at barricades used by the shooters.

The wagons slowed down near the Joy Club and the thrower was about to lob his deadly load up on to the verandah when Ford noticed a woman standing at an upstairs window.

'Don't!' he shouted and the man stopped mid-throw. 'There's women in there.'

Without hesitation, he threw it away from the group and into the vacant area beyond the end of the street. It exploded violently sending a geyser of earth into the air.

'That was close,' Krouse called out.

'Get them turned!' Ford shouted. 'We're goin' back. How many sticks have you got left?'

'Four,' answered Allen.

'All right, let's go!'

'What the hell was that?' Beck said, coughing.

'The bastards are using dynamite,' Cordis said, slapping dust from his clothes.

'But they'll destroy the town if they keep doin' that,' Beck pointed out.

'I think that's the idea.'

Both men were covered in grime from head to toe from their proximity to the blast that took out the front of the Royal Palace. Beck's shirt was torn across the back, exposing an angry red stripe across the bare skin.

Ike Cordis had a torn shirtsleeve and a thin trickle of blood on his brow where a sliver of wood had scored the flesh. He looked along the street and saw the devastation that the first pass had left in its wake. They needed to do something quickly otherwise all would be lost.

One of his gunmen shouted a warning. 'They're comin' back!'

'All right, let's take cover again,' Cordis said, not wanting to be exposed to another mind-numbing blast. 'Sam, we need to stop them throwing those powder sticks.'

'I'll do it,' Beck assured his boss. 'Count on it.'

The second run came on with a rumbling of hoofs and wagon wheels. The gunfire recommenced and then an explosion blew up part of the boardwalk, taking out two hidden shooters outside of the saddlery.

As Ford rode past on the blue roan, Cordis took a bead on him and squeezed the trigger. The outlaw boss smiled in satisfaction when he saw the marshal flinch as the bullet struck his right side. Ford swayed in the saddle but stayed upright and continued to ride.

The first wagon rumbled past; the cowhands in the back firing relentlessly. Bullets smacked into the debris field behind which Cordis and Beck had taken cover. Another explosion rocked Absaroka Street, inflicting more damage. The body of a concealed shooter was flung violently into the air, landing sickeningly in an almost unrecognizable heap.

'Damn it, Sam, stop that son of a bitch!' Cordis cursed.

Sighting along the barrel of his six-gun, Beck drew a bead on the man in the back of the second wagon. His arm was raised and he was about to lob another stick with a lit fuse towards a large false-fronted building.

Beck fired and the man cried out then collapsed to the wagon bed. The sputtering stick of dynamite dropped from of sight behind the wagon. No sooner had it hit the ground than it blew. The wagon took the full force of the explosion, shattering it like matchwood. The driver was killed instantly by the blast, but somehow the horses escaped unscathed and bolted on, trailing reins and wagon tongue.

'That showed him,' satisfaction evident in Beck's voice.

When Ford and the others reached their starting point just outside of town, he dismounted and reloaded the Winchester. His side throbbed and he could feel the blood running freely down his side.

'You've been shot,' Krouse said aloud as he approached Ford. 'Are you OK?'

Ford winced. 'I'll live. How are we doin'?'

'We lost three men,' Krouse informed him. 'Smith, Allen, and James.'

Ford nodded grimly. 'All right, let's clear them out.'

Ford led them forward into what was fast beginning to resemble the place that Serenity had become known as: Hell. Orange flames had taken hold of the tinder dry wood that the shops and other buildings along Absaroka Street were constructed of. That, coupled with the piles of rubble and the dead bodies, would make a person believe that cannons had fired upon the town.

As Ford and the others began to advance along the street, the fires were forcing Cordis' hired guns away from the buildings and out into the open. Gunfire erupted once again as the two forces engaged in deadly combat.

Ahead, three men broke into the relative safety of Absaroka Street. They stopped when they saw the advancing men and brought their weapons up to fire. The flat reports of gunshots cracked out. One of the cowboys beside Ford cursed and went down with a bullet in his leg.

Ford wasn't sure, but he thought that he detected a hint of disappointment in his voice too.

'Find him some cover,' Ford snapped as he shot down another of Cordis' men.

With the wounded man now placed behind a water trough, they continued to advance through the town. The dynamite seemed to have taken the fight out of the defenders and only a few die-hards remained.

'Split up,' Ford ordered them.

He walked along the street with a cowhand called Harold Timms. They kept an even pace, scanning their surroundings as they went on. Ford could feel the radiated heat from the flames against the skin of his face. A building that had once been the Cattleman's Association office collapsed in a shower of sparks and leaping flames. For the first time since the battle had started, Ford began to question his method in trying to defeat Cordis.

'Too late to go back now,' he muttered.

The sudden appearance of two figures that broke from cover and moved into the centre of Absaroka Street startled Ford as they brought up their weapons and opened fire. Beside Ford, Timms cried out with pain as a bullet took him high in the chest. Ford fired back and saw the second man throw his arms up and fall backward.

Before the first man fired his gun again, Ford knew he

was in trouble. Two shots cracked out and he felt a burning pain in his left leg as a bullet tore into his thigh. He collapsed into a heap as the wounded appendage refused to support his weight.

Another shot sounded and a bright light flashed in Ford's head as the slug burned along the left side of his face, just above the hairline. He fell on to his back, head spinning, and unconsciousness threatened to consume him. Overhead, great plumes of dirty brown smoke started to blot out the sky above.

Footsteps pierced the foggy haze of Ford's brain and he turned his head to meet the sound. He stared at the figure that loomed over him but his eyes wouldn't focus. Ford blinked to clear his vision and momentarily the sneering face of Ike Cordis swam into view.

'You son of a bitch. You've ruined everything,' he snarled and raised the six-gun in his fist.

The thunder of gunfire crashed out and everything went black for Ford.

CHAPTER 18

The first thing Ford became aware of was the throbbing in his head. It felt like miners were inside trying to dig their way out with picks. He moaned and lifted his hand to the place where the bullet had bitten him. His fingers came away sticky with blood.

Then it struck him; he was still alive. He opened his eyes and saw the outline of a figure kneeling close to him. At first, he thought it was Cordis, but the killer didn't have red hair, and as his vision cleared further, Eddie's smiling face became visible. Her face and clothes were blackened with soot.

'Keep still while I tie this bandage off,' she said to him.

'What happened?'

'Ike Cordis shot you.'

Then Ford remembered. 'Where is he?'

Eddie nodded to his left.

Ford turned his head and he saw the figure of Cordis to his left, lying on his back, dead. He looked back at Eddie.

She shrugged her shoulders. 'I couldn't let him kill you, could I?'

'For that, I thank you, but what are you doin' here?'

'I followed you and waited for a chance to get Cordis for what he did,' she told him.

'How long was I out?'

'Ten minutes, not long.'

'The others?'

'Krouse came past and said that the others capitulated and they chased them out of town. I guess once Cordis died, they had nothing left to fight for. Can you get up?'

With help from Eddie, Ford managed to climb to his feet, swayed a little when pressure was applied to his wounded leg and then steadied himself.

'When we find somewhere better, I'll look at those other wounds of yours.'

'You look like you've been through hell, by the way,' Ford deadpanned.

'Speak for yourself,' she retorted with a smile.

'Pick my rifle up for me?'

'Are you wounded or something?'

Biting back a wave of pain, Ford said, 'You could say that.'

Rolling her eyes, Eddie bent and picked up the Winchester. 'Here, you need to toughen up a little, Marshal.'

'Is that an offer to help?'

An alarmed expression sprang to Eddie's face. 'Hell, no. You're too much trouble for me.'

Ford laughed and immediately wished he hadn't.

'Come on,' Eddie said, moving to his side, 'lean on me and we'll find a place to look at you.'

They were making their way along the street through

the smoke haze when Ford noticed the three men leading their horses along Absaroka Street.

'Aw shoot,' Ford said. 'This will go well.'

'What's the matter?' Eddie asked.

Ford nodded in the direction of the three men.

'Who are they?'

'See that feller in the middle?'

'Yes.'

'He's United States Marshal Bass Reeves. My pa.'

'Oh.'

'Yeah, "oh" is right.'

Ford and Eddie stopped in front of the three lawmen. He gave his father a wry smile and said, 'Hey, Bass, where you been?'

The look on Reeves' face said it all and in a low rumbling voice he asked, 'What the *hell* have you done?'

'How did he take it?' Eddie asked as she started to tend his wounded side.

'About as well as I expected him to,' Ford told her. 'And he didn't fire me so I guess that's somethin'. He's talkin' to Krouse at the minute.'

Behind them, the main street still burned orange, although the flames were beginning to abate. The sun was about gone behind the mountains and in the twilight, Ford suddenly felt like a large weight had been lifted from his shoulders.

'Where to for you now?' Eddie asked.

'Into exile I'm afraid,' Ford told her. 'Bass is sending me to Texas.'

'What's in Texas?'

'More bad men I guess.'

Eddie smiled. 'Well, it's lucky for you that I'm headed for Texas.'

Ford smiled. 'Yes, indeed. Very lucky.'